There was a ... door and a m... 'Room Servic...

Becky gathered h... ...around her and padded across to open the door, her eyes growing wider with shock to see Jack standing there.

'Did someone call for large fries, a double cheeseburger, a Coke and a chocolate and blueberry cheesecake?' he asked.

'Why are you here?'

'Can't you guess?'

He stepped towards her and took one of her hands, and gently unpeeled her locked fingers, one by one.

'W-what are you doing?'

He pressed a soft kiss into the middle of her palm and closed her fingers back over it, his eyes still holding hers.

'I'm telling you that I love you,' he said.

'I don't believe you.'

'Then I'll have to find another way to convince you,' he said, and took her other hand and did the same to it. 'Convinced yet?'

A&E DRAMA

Blood pressure is high and pulses are racing in these fast-paced dramatic stories from Mills & Boon® Medical Romance™. They'll move a mountain to save a life in an emergency, be they the crash team, emergency doctors, or paramedics. There are lots of critical engagements amongst the high tensions and emotional passions in these exciting stories of lives and loves at risk!

Recent titles by the same author:

Medical Romance™
HER PROTECTOR IN ER

> Melanie also writes for Modern Romance™—
> look out for her latest—coming soon!

Modern Romance™
BACK IN HER HUSBAND'S BED
THE GREEK'S CONVENIENT WIFE
THE ITALIAN'S MISTRESS

A SURGEON WORTH WAITING FOR

BY
MELANIE MILBURNE

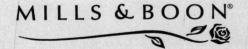

MILLS & BOON®

First published in Great Britain 2005
Harlequin Mills & Boon Limited,
Eton House, 18-24 Paradise Road, Richmond, Surrey TW9 1SR

© Melanie Milburne 2005

ISBN 0 263 84349 1

Set in Times Roman 10 on 11 pt.
03-1205-53496

Printed and bound in Spain
by Litografia Rosés, S.A., Barcelona

CHAPTER ONE

'WHERE the hell is the anaesthetist?' Jack Colcannon growled as he looked at the clock on the wall for the fifth frustrating time. 'I have a huge operating list and I don't want to start late yet again.'

'Becky should be here soon,' Gwen Taylor, the scrub nurse, said. 'Anyway, if there was a problem she would have phoned in by now.'

Jack grunted as he turned towards the theatre tearoom. Rebecca Baxter might be his best friend's younger sister but working with her was proving to be a nightmare in more ways than one. Sure, she was a good anaesthetist—in fact, probably one of the best he'd worked with during the whole time he'd been at St Patrick's—but something about her always seemed to get under his skin.

He poured himself a cup of coffee and, taking it across to the window, looked at the view of the Sydney skyline in the distance. The summer sun was beating down relentlessly, and with only three weeks to go until Christmas he could almost feel the hectic pulse of the city as swarms of shoppers went about their frantic business.

He shifted his gaze and looked down to where he'd parked his new car earlier that morning. He'd taken delivery of it the week before and couldn't help a small smile of satisfaction as he thought of the power and thrust under the bonnet, the surge of speed that sent him backwards in the leather-clad seat as soon as his foot hit the throttle.

He took another sip of his coffee and was just about to turn away from the window when he saw a bright pink Volkswagen Beetle swing into the car park and begin the hunt for a parking spot.

Rebecca Baxter tried to nudge between two cars in the shade of a spindly tree, but after three attempts to reverse, she gave up and chugged a little further along to where Jack's car was parked. Putting on her indicator, she began to reverse into the tight space behind.

His fingers automatically tightened around his cup, his breath stilling in his chest as he watched her manoeuvre the car into position, the relief when she did it without touching the immaculate paintwork of his car sending his halted breath out on a whoosh.

'So there is a god after all,' he murmured as he began to turn away from the window.

The sound of metal crunching against metal made him swing back so quickly his coffee went in a dark brown arc across the floor, and his mouth dropped open as he looked down below.

'Oops!' Becky winced at her misjudgement of the clutch release, quickly scanning the car park to see if anyone had witnessed her error. To her immense relief no one had appeared to notice.

She got out and inspected her car. Thankfully there wasn't a single scratch.

But as for Jack Colcannon's car…

She bit her lip, took a calming breath, and turned around to look at it. She knew how particular Jack was over things, and not just his car.

His brand-new car, she reminded herself with a sinking feeling in the pit of her stomach as her eyes went to the nasty dent in his bumper. She bent over to peer at it. Was that a tiny bit of pink paint?

She sensed him coming before she heard him, which was saying something for her sixth sense, as he was practically bawling her out from the front door of the hospital, way across the car park.

'What the hell do you think you're doing?' He strode towards her angrily, his theatre gear plastered to his tall muscled frame by the hot stiff breeze that was coming in from the west. 'Who in God's name taught you how to park?'

Becky lifted her chin and faced his furious green gaze with an equanimity she didn't quite feel. 'My brother Ben did, and, if I remember correctly…' she gave him a pointed little look from beneath her lashes '…you even once took me out for a quick park yourself.'

Jack set his jaw.

How like her to remind him of the one time he had lost all control with her. More than a decade had passed since that sweltering afternoon when he'd looked down at the full curve of her pouting seventeen-year-old mouth and…

'Anyway,' she continued before he could think of a suitable retort, 'it's the tiniest, weeniest little dent. Nothing to make such a fuss about.'

He sent her a withering look and squatted down in front of his car to inspect the damage, running his long tanned fingers over the bent metal.

Becky felt her stomach muscles instinctively tighten. As much as she hated to admit it, Jack had the most amazing hands. She watched as they moved over the bumper, trying not to think of how they would feel moving over her skin, over her face, tracing the line of her mouth.

She had felt his mouth on hers—just the once, but the memory of it had stayed with her as if it had happened yesterday. Sometimes she felt as if she could still taste him when she swept her tongue across the surface of her lips…

He straightened to his full height and turned to look down at her, his mouth tight with tension.

'The whole thing will have to be replaced.'

'What?' She stared at him in heart-tripping alarm. 'The whole *car*?'

He rolled his eyes heavenwards, his tone clipped with biting sarcasm. 'No. Not the whole car, Rebecca, just the bumper.'

Becky hated the way he made the full use of her name sound like an insult. No one else did it, just him.

She would have hitched her chin up another notch but she

was already craning her neck to maintain eye contact as it was. He was taller than her six-foot-one brother by about three inches and, no matter how often she wore heels to work, her five-foot-five frame still barely came up to his broad shoulders.

'You know something, Jack?' she said with a cutting edge to her voice. 'You really should have booked in for that emergency personality bypass by now. You're really starting to annoy me, and that is not a good thing.'

'Oh, really?' He gave her a glittering look. 'Well, for your information, Dr Baxter, you rate pretty high on my annoyance Richter scale, too. My operating list is now going to be at least an hour late because of you breezing in here like this. What were you doing to make you so late? Your Christmas shopping?'

Becky glared at him, her mouth thinned out with anger. 'I had a flat tyre.'

'Another one?' His expression was disbelieving. 'That makes—let me see now…' He held up his hand and counted on his long fingers as if speaking to a small child. 'One last week, one on Monday and now another one today.'

She pursed her lips and folded her arms without answering.

'Come on, Rebecca,' he said. 'Can't you think of something a little better than that? What about a granny's or distant great-aunt's funeral or something?'

'I told you the truth.' She bit the words out hard. 'I have had three flat tyres in six days. It's costing me a fortune to have them fixed.'

'Yeah, well, it's costing the government a packet to keep this public hospital up and running, and if we don't get this list started immediately the CEO will be on my back yet again about the ever-increasing waiting list.'

Becky turned away to get her bag off the front seat, her teeth catching her bottom lip momentarily. She had never had car trouble before, but now it seemed as if something was going wrong every single day. Even the brakes had felt a little spongy when she'd pulled into the car park, though she'd had the car serviced less than ten days ago.

She hoisted her bag over one shoulder and flicked the remote to lock the car, turning back to glance up at Jack, who was watching her silently.

'I'll pay for the damages,' she said, brushing past him to make her way towards the entrance. 'Just send me the bill.'

Jack frowned as her heels click-clacked across the car park, her small figure disappearing through the automatic doors of the hospital as if the building were swallowing her whole.

He gave a rough-edged sigh, ran a hand through his dark hair and followed her into the building.

It was going to be another one of those days, he was sure.

'Betadine prep, Gwen, please,' Jack said, once the first patient was anaesthetised. Gwen handed him the Betadine and he applied it to the abdomen liberally before handing the dish and applicator back. The patient was draped and the diathermy and sucker set up.

'Scalpel.'

He made a midline incision in the abdomen of sixty-five-year-old Hugh Williams, who had a sigmoid colon cancer.

'Rebecca, the usual antibiotics and heparin, please,' he said.

'Already given,' Becky answered. 'Can we tip him a little head down, please? He's a vasculopath and a little hypotensive at the moment.'

'Yes, all right, head down a bit. Diathermy, Gwen,' Jack said as he completed the opening of the abdomen.

He inserted a Balfour self-retaining retractor and carried out an exploration of the abdomen to assess the extent of the cancer, his frown behind his protective mask deepening as he concentrated.

'No liver metastases but the primary is stuck to the left pelvic wall.' He addressed his registrar assistant, Robert Caulfield. 'It's going to have to be dissected off the iliac vessels and ureter.'

Half an hour later Jack spoke again. 'This tumour is very adherent, Robert—I'm taking it off the iliacs now... *Shoot!* Vascular clamp, Gwen. The tumour is into the common iliac and we have a hole in the artery. Robert, compress the bleeding with packs till we clamp the artery.'

'What are you guys doing down there?' Becky asked, her eyes still on the monitor. 'His BP has dropped right off.'

'We're into the common iliac artery and losing blood fast,' Jack answered. 'Where's that clamp, Gwen?'

'Coming, Jack,' Gwen said. 'We weren't expecting to need vascular extras.'

'Mr Williams has got marginal cardiac function,' Becky informed them. 'Either you stop the bleeding or we're going to be in trouble soon. I'm putting in an extra IV line and starting colloid. Did you cross-match blood, Rob?'

'Just grouped and held, Dr Baxter,' Robert answered. 'We don't normally cross-match for a sigmoid colectomy.'

'Right, then, I'm taking blood for an urgent cross-match. Jack, I'm getting in O-negative blood. I can't hold him on crystalloid any longer.'

'Whatever,' Jack said tightly. 'Just keep him in there till I can clamp this artery.'

'The Satinsky vascular clamp is here, Jack,' Gwen informed him.

'Hold back the sigmoid mesentery and get that sucker in there to clear the field while I clamp, Robert. Ready. Now, suck, retract.'

Jack applied the clamp to the common iliac artery and the bleeding stopped. He allowed himself a small sigh of relief and addressed Becky. 'Bleeding has stopped, Rebecca. How is he?'

'Hypotensive but holding in there. I've got O-negative blood pumping in, looks about two and a half litres of blood loss, but if you've got the bleeding stopped we can manage it.'

'Good. Vascular suture, Gwen.'

Jack repaired the hole in the common iliac artery, taking care not to damage the left ureter. The sigmoid colon was then freed and resected.

'Blood supply to the bowel ends looks good. I'm doing a

hand-sewn anastomosis. Gwen, outer 2/0 black silk and inner 2/0 chromic catgut.'

'No stapler, then?' Gwen queried.

'No, the anastomosis is too far from the rectum.' Jack went on to complete the anastomosis and close the mesenteric defect.

'You can close up, Robert, no drains,' he said, stepping away from the patient. 'Everything all right your end, Rebecca?'

'He's stable and good BP,' Becky said, exchanging relieved glances with the anaesthetic nurse beside her.

Jack left the operating theatre to write up his operation notes on Mr Williams as the registrar completed the closure of the abdomen.

'What's eating Jack this morning?' Julie, the anaesthetic nurse, asked the rest of the theatre staff. 'He came in growling like a bear first thing.'

'He was on call last night,' Gwen said, handing Robert a skin stapler. 'A twenty-year-old road trauma victim died in Theatre. He did everything he could but it wasn't enough. The kid bled out.'

Becky felt a wave of shame go through her for the way she'd spoken to him in the car park. She of all people knew the stress of losing a patient, how it ate at you in the middle of yet another sleepless night as you agonised over what could have or should have been done, even if there had been a chance.

She looked at the still unconscious Mr Williams and sighed. He was one of the lucky ones. His family would see him in a few hours, a little worse for wear but hopefully with a good few more years left to live, thanks to Jack's meticulous skill and care.

She followed the orderlies as they wheeled the patient out to Recovery, checking that Mr Williams was responding to voice before returning to Theatre to get ready for the next case.

'What was that ruckus about in the car park this morning?' Gwen asked once Becky came back.

'You *heard* that?' Becky gave her a startled look.

Gwen smiled as she stripped off her sterile gown and stuffed it in the laundry bin. 'What is it with you two? That stunt you just pulled off with Mr Williams proves just how well you can work together. Why can't you bury whatever hatchet there is and kiss and make up?'

'It would take an entire peace congress to sort out the mess,' Becky answered ruefully. 'Jack's had a chip on his shoulder about me for years, which up until this morning was the size of the Sydney Cricket Ground, but it has now just grown to include Centennial Park and Fox Studios as well.'

'Uh-oh.' Gwen's face screwed up in an I-know-this-is-going-to-be-bad grimace. 'Whatever did you do?'

'I ran into the back of his car. His brand-new car.'

Gwen whistled through her teeth. 'Not good.'

'Definitely not good,' Becky agreed.

'Why were you late in the first place?' Gwen asked.

'I had another flat tyre.'

Gwen's brows rose. 'What have you been doing, girl, parking on pins and needles?'

'Not that I know of.' She sighed as she looked at the wall where the patient list was situated. 'But I do seem to be having a run of bad luck.'

'Have you heard from your parents?' Gwen tactfully changed the subject.

'Not by phone but I've had a few emails,' Becky said, turning back to face her. 'They're doing a Greek Island tour and once that's finished they're moving on to spend Christmas in Prague.'

'What about your brother Ben? What's he up to?'

Becky wasn't sure how to answer. She hadn't heard from her older brother in weeks, which, considering his line of work as a special operations cop, wasn't all that unusual, but somehow just lately she'd felt increasingly uneasy, as if she could sense he was in some sort of danger.

'He's away on some assignment or other,' she said somewhat evasively. 'You know what thirty-four-year-old men are like. They don't like to be tied down for too long.'

'Speaking of thirty-four-year-old men…' Gwen's voice dropped to an undertone as she nodded towards the doctors' room where Jack had gone earlier. 'Has Mr Grumpy got himself a new girlfriend yet? It's been months since he broke up with Marcia.'

'I'm not sure…' Becky answered, shifting her gaze.

'That's probably why he's so out of sorts,' Gwen said reflectively. 'All those surging hormones of his are all dressed up and have nowhere to go.'

Becky was quite relieved when it was time to prepare the next patient. She was sure Jack wouldn't appreciate her discussing his hormones with the theatre staff.

'That was good work with Mr Williams,' Jack told her as he came in scrubbed up for the next procedure. 'I thought we were going to lose him.'

Becky wasn't used to his praise, and even though it had been handed to her somewhat grudgingly, she still felt a warm wave of something indefinable pass through her at his words and brief glance in her direction.

'Thanks,' she said, and turned to the patient she was monitoring.

'Right,' Jack said, turning to the rest of the gathered staff, 'let's get this mastectomy under way.'

The rest of the list passed routinely, the mastectomy followed by a laparoscopic adrenalectomy, thyroidectomy and two laparoscopic cholecystectomies before theatre management pulled the plug on the last case. No time overruns were being permitted, and any cases left over had to go onto the next scheduled list.

Becky could see the frustration on Jack's face as he stripped off his protective gear. He was a hard-working surgeon who hated the bureaucratic red tape that tied up the public operating system into neat orderly nine-to-five working days.

She'd often wondered why he didn't shift his skills to the

private sector, where the financial gains were far more substantial. His father, Emery Colcannon, was one of Sydney's best-known private cosmetic surgeons and it had always seemed a little strange to her that Jack, his only child, had chosen to become a staff specialist in a cash-strapped public hospital.

But, then, who was she to talk? Here was she, a twenty-nine-year-old staff anaesthetist who hadn't quite made up her mind whether to take the step into a lucrative private practice arrangement or continue as she was.

Maybe she and Jack weren't so different after all, she thought as she followed the last patient out to Recovery.

'Jack?' Becky entered the doctors' room half an hour later.

He looked up, closing the folder he'd been writing in and pushed it to one side as he leaned back in his chair. 'Yes?'

She closed the door softly behind her, trying not to be put off by his curt and dismissive attitude as her eyes met his.

'I'm sorry for being so rude to you this morning,' she said, looking down at her hands resting on the back of the chair she'd instinctively grabbed for support. 'I didn't realise you'd had a bad night and I wanted to—'

He got to his feet in one fluid movement, which seemed to instantly shrink the size of the room. She lifted her head and encountered his hard green gaze, her stomach doing a little reshuffle in the process.

'If you think you're going to get out of a damages claim then you are very much mistaken,' he said. 'I've already contacted the assessor. I'll post you the bill as soon as I receive it.'

'I wasn't apologising about the car,' she said. 'That was truly an accident. But I am sorry about the way I reacted. You were upset and I didn't think—'

'Leave it, Rebecca.' He picked up the folder from the desk. 'I don't need your apologies or your excuses. What I need right now is the flat surface of a bed for at least six hours— seven would be heaven.'

'I—I didn't really mean the bit about the personality by-pass,' she said as he strode towards the door.

Jack turned around to look at her, his hand still on the door-knob, his expression cynical. 'Didn't you?'

But before she could answer the door had opened and closed, and all that was left of him in the room was the faint trace of his aftershave lingering in the air that she began to draw somewhat raggedly into her lungs.

CHAPTER TWO

BECKY wasn't sure what woke her during the night. She wasn't normally a restless sleeper but she hadn't really settled all that well into the rented flat in Randwick. It was on a noisy street, and late-night revellers often wandered past, kicking over bins or vandalising cars.

She'd been saving for her own property but real estate was expensive in the inner suburbs, and she'd been hesitant about committing herself to borrowing such a large sum of money until she finally decided what career direction to take.

She lay listening for a moment without moving a muscle, doing her best to keep her breathing steady as she strained to hear whatever sound had woken her.

There it was again—the sounds of stealthy footsteps coming down the hall towards her bedroom, making every single hair lift up on her scalp in fear.

Becky didn't like to think of herself as a coward, but her level of expertise in terms of self-defence was of the vase-and-baseball-bat type. The only trouble was that her one and only vase was full of bright yellow roses in the kitchen, and she didn't, and never had, possessed a baseball bat.

She slipped out of bed as quietly as she could and, scrabbling around in the dark, picked up one of her shoes off the floor, holding the four-inch heel poised as she waited by the side of the door, her heart pounding like a hammer behind the wall of her chest.

Her breath stalled when the bedroom door was slowly pushed open. She flattened herself against the wall, wishing she could see through the darkness properly, but she'd pulled the blind down before going to bed in order to block out the streetlights. The tiny finger of light that found its way underneath the edge of the blind was only enough to fill the room with leaping shadows, which did absolutely nothing to ease her terror.

She clutched her shoe a little tighter for reassurance but her hands were damp with increasing panic and she knew it wouldn't take much for her drop it and run off screaming like the coward she was.

Ben would think it pathetic of her, of course. When the bravery genes were handed out in the Baxter family, her big brother had turned up first and taken the lot.

She watched in silent horror as a tall dark figure approached her bed slowly, cautiously, as if expecting her to leap out of the jumble of bedcovers and fire a weapon at him. The intruder switched on a tiny torch about the size of a pen and shone it over the bed and bedside table before turning around and training it right on her face.

'G-get out of my b-bedroom or I'll shoot,' she said, holding her shoe out like a pistol.

She thought she heard a snicker of laughter but her heart was making such a racket and there was a heavy roaring in her ears, so she wasn't sure if she imagined it. The intruder wore a full balaclava and gloves, his tight-fitting dark clothes making him appear all the more menacing.

'W-what do you want?' she asked, desperately hoping he wasn't the serial sex offender the police were searching for.

The intruder didn't answer but stood with his torchlight trained on her eyes so she couldn't see. Becky could feel herself cracking. She wasn't used to this amount of adrenalin flooding her system. Give her a flat line heart monitor any day. She could deal with that. But this was something else. Her legs were giving up on her and her hands were shaking so much the shoe dropped to the floor at her feet with a soft little thud.

The intruder turned off the torch and melted away in the darkness, closing the bedroom door with a tiny click as he left. Becky stood for endless seconds, unable to believe he'd gone without harming her, relief flowing through her like a tidal wave when she heard the front door open and close on his exit.

She lunged for the phone by her bed and pressed in the emergency code, her heart ramming her breastbone as the operator answered.

'Police! Get me the police!' she cried.

She was switched through to the local police and as soon as the officer on the end of the line spoke she blurted out her story. 'There was a man in my bedroom! You have to get over here and catch him.'

'What is your name, ma'am?' the officer asked.

'My name is— Hey, didn't you hear me?' Becky said. 'There was an intruder in my bedroom! He's probably still in the area!'

'What's your address?' the officer asked in the sort of bored tone that suggested he'd had one too many of this type of call that evening.

She forced herself to take a calming breath, answering in a controlled tone, 'I live at 4/56 Marigold Place, Randwick.'

'And your name?'

'Beck—Rebecca Baxter,' she said. 'Dr Rebecca Baxter.'

'I'll send a car as soon as one is available,' the officer said. 'In the meantime, is there anyone you could call to stay with you until we send someone over to take a statement?'

The only person Becky wanted to call was her brother, but when he was on assignment he was unreachable even by email. During those times it was like he had completely disappeared off the face of the earth. Her parents were on the other side of the earth, which left her with the last man on earth she wanted to call. But he lived close by, and her parents and brother had always insisted he was just like one of the family…

'Yes,' she answered a little lamely.

'Call them now, and hopefully our guys will get there before he or she does,' the officer said.

Becky stared at the phone for a moment before pressing in

Jack's home number, which she knew by heart from all the times she'd had to call him on patient-related matters.

'Colcannon,' Jack said somewhat groggily.

Becky glanced at the bedside clock and winced when she saw it was just after three a.m.

'Jack? It's me, Becky.'

She heard him smother a groan and the protest of the bed as he repositioned himself.

'Rebecca. I take it this isn't a social call?' She heard the sound of his hand scraping over the unshaven roughness of his jaw. 'Please, don't tell me one of today's patients has had a major bleed or—'

'There was a man in my bedroom,' she interrupted him bluntly.

There was a tiny silence.

'And you felt the sudden need to confess that to me?' There was more than a hint of satire in his tone.

'He was wearing a balaclava,' she bit out, stung by his mockery.

'Kinky.'

She let out her breath in a hiss. 'Will you listen to me, for God's sake? I told you there was an intruder in my flat and you're making a big joke out of it and I...I...' She gulped back a sob.

Jack bolted upright, brushing his hair out of his eyes, his hand tightening on the receiver. 'An intruder? What sort of intruder?'

'T-the usual s-sort, dressed all in black with gloves and—'

'Hell, Becky,' he said as his gut clenched painfully. 'Are you all right? Did he hurt you, or—?'

'I—I'm fine,' she said. 'The police are on their way.'

'I'll be right over,' he said, reaching for his neatly folded trousers. 'Stay there and don't answer the door unless you are sure it's me or the police, got that?'

'Y-yes.' She gave him the address, and put down the phone, and chewed her nails and waited.

*   *   *

She wasn't all that surprised when Jack arrived before the police. She heard his car roar up the street and watched as he parked behind her Beetle with the effortless ease she'd always envied.

She opened the door to his knock and stood before him uncertainly.

'You called me B-Becky,' she said and, stepping towards him, promptly burst into tears.

Jack held her trembling form against him without speaking. He knew she wouldn't have called him if Ben or her parents had been in town, but somehow knowing she'd thought of him as next in line made him feel inexplicably warm inside.

He'd always done his best to keep her at arm's length, not wanting to compromise his relationship to her brother with an affair with her that would have no future. He wasn't planning on getting married and Becky was nothing if not the marrying type. She'd already been engaged three times as it was. He'd seen the magazines she pored over during long operations where the monitors did half the work for her. Brides and babies were her thing. She even had names picked out, for heaven's sake!

No.

He wasn't going down the same pathway of his parents who, even twenty-four years after their acrimonious divorce, were still not on speaking terms. For years they had used him as a go-between until he'd finally put a stop to it by limiting his contact to birthdays and Christmas. Thank God he was on call this year, which meant for once he wouldn't have to choose between them.

The police announced their arrival and Jack eased Becky out of his arms to answer the door. He stood to one side as Becky gave her statement, his blood chilling as he heard the details.

'Did he say anything to you?' the female officer asked, pen in hand.

'No.'

'Nothing at all?'

'I thought I heard him laugh.'

The officers exchanged glances.

'What sort of laugh?' the male officer asked, looking at her intently.

'A sort of little chuckle.' She gave them a grimace of embarrassment. 'I might have imagined it. I was very frightened…'

'How long have you lived here?'

'About four months,' Becky said. 'I used to live in Mosman but my flatmate got married. I had to find somewhere else to live in a hurry.'

'Have you any known enemies?' the female officer asked. 'Perhaps an ex-boyfriend or partner who might have found it hard to let go?'

If only, Becky thought wryly. Every one of her ex-fiancés had had absolutely no difficulty whatsoever in letting her go. Two of them hadn't even waited around long enough for her to return their engagement rings.

'No.'

'What about through work?' the male officer asked, glancing at his notes. 'You said you're a doctor. Have you ever had a patient who was overly interested in you?'

'I'm an anaesthetist.' Becky's mouth twisted ruefully. 'Apart from my initial assessment before surgery, my patients are all asleep.'

'What about a colleague?' the female officer asked. 'Anyone you don't particularly like?'

Becky was very conscious of Jack's silent figure standing close by. She shifted from foot to foot and ran her tongue over her lips, but she had difficulty locating her voice.

'Dr Baxter?' the officer prompted, watching her closely.

Becky shook her head. 'No, there's no one I don't get on with.'

'Do you have anything of particular value in your flat that the intruder might have been after? Drugs or cash, or a prescription pad or jewellery?'

'I have a prescription pad in my bag but no cash or jewellery of any value. He didn't seem to be looking for anything. He just stood there, looking at me.'

'Do you think you'd recognise this man in a line-up?' the female constable asked.

Becky caught her lip between her teeth for a moment as she thought about it. 'I'm not sure.'

'Did he have any distinguishing features?'

'He was tall,' Becky said.

'How tall?'

'Six foot or so.' She looked at Jack briefly. 'Not as tall as Jack but similar build. It was hard to see—it was dark—and he was dressed in black clothing, including gloves and bala-clava.'

'Yes, we haven't got any prints off the doorknobs so he certainly knew what he was doing,' the female constable said. 'Does anyone apart from you have a key to this apartment?'

Becky shook her head. 'No, not that I know of.'

'You haven't given anyone a set of keys at any time?' The constable flicked her gaze in Jack's direction before returning to look at her. 'Perhaps when someone was staying over for the night?'

'No.' Becky felt her cheeks grow warm with embarrassment. She hadn't even had a girlfriend stay for a sleep-over, let alone a man. Hell, how desperate and dateless had she become?

'Well, if you think of anything else, please don't hesitate to contact us,' the male officer said. 'And, of course, always lock your door and windows. We're still hunting for a serial sex offender and until we find him you can't be too careful.'

'Right.' Becky gave them both a weak smile as she led the way to the door. 'Thank you for your help.'

'No problem.' The male officer met Jack's eyes. 'It might be an idea if you stayed the rest of the night with her, just to be on the safe side.'

'Sure,' Jack found himself agreeing.

'And it would be a good idea to get the locks changed as soon as possible,' the female officer advised. 'There was no sign of a forced entry so unless you inadvertently left the door unlocked, this guy probably has a key.'

The door closed on the officers' exit and Becky turned to look at Jack, her chocolate brown eyes still shadowed with residual fear. 'You don't have to stay. I'll be fine.'

Jack drew in a breath of resignation. 'Your brother would kill me if I let anything happen to you in his absence.' He scraped a hand through his dark hair, leaving finger-sized comb marks in the shiny black strands. 'Not to mention your parents.'

Becky felt a little resentful that he was only offering to stay on behalf of her family. Why couldn't he be doing it for his own reasons?

'I'm sure you have much better things to do than babysit your best mate's kid sister,' she said, folding her arms across her chest.

'As long as I can lie flat and sleep, I don't care if I'm babysitting Godzilla's god-daughter.' He looked around the room, his gaze coming to rest on her small sofa. 'I don't suppose you have a spare bedroom in this matchbox of an apartment, do you?'

'I have one bed,' she said, her mouth pulled tight. 'Mine.'

'Want to toss for it?' he asked, taking a coin out of his pocket and turning it over in his fingers.

Becky's mouth tightened even further.

'I'll take that as a no,' he said. Glancing at the sofa, he added over one shoulder, 'Have you got a spare pillow I could borrow?'

She went to her room, snatched one off her bed and brought it back to him, shoving it at his chest. 'Here. Sweet dreams,' she said. 'I hope you don't snore.'

'I haven't had any complaints so far,' he said. 'What about you?'

'What about me?'

A small smile lurked around the edges of his mouth. 'Have any of your previous partners complained about the noise you make in bed?'

She forced herself to meet his glinting green gaze, even though her cheeks felt as if someone had blowtorched them from the inside. 'No complaints so far.'

'Well, then…' He started to unbutton his shirt. 'Do you think we should leave a light on in case Mr Balaclava thinks about returning?'

Becky suppressed a gulp as he shrugged off his shirt, the smooth tanned muscles of his chest making her eyes widen to the size of dinner plates. She'd thought Ben was fit, but Jack had obviously been working out. His pectoral muscles looked as if he'd been bench-pressing an entire road train with a couple of Hummers thrown in for good measure.

'I…I don't know…' Her gaze dipped to the flat plane of his stomach, the ripple of abdominal muscles making her instinctively suck in her tummy. She raised her eyes back to his with an effort. 'What do you think?'

Jack glanced at his watch. 'Lights or no lights, I think if we don't get to sleep within the next twenty minutes it won't be worth going to bed at all. I have a gym session at six a.m. and residents' rounds at seven-thirty.' He took off his shoes and socks and began to undo his belt when he suddenly thought better of it and let his hands fall away.

'You must be so tired.' She gave him an apologetic look, her hands twisting in front of her. 'I shouldn't have called you but you live the closest…'

'Don't worry about it,' he said lying down on the sofa, his long trouser-clad legs hanging over the end. 'As I said, Ben would lynch me if I didn't stand in for him as honorary big brother.'

She gave him an imitation of a smile. This was probably not the time to tell him she had never quite seen him in a brotherly light. That one kiss twelve years ago had changed that—permanently.

'Well, goodnight, then,' she said, turning for the door.

'Goodnight, Rebecca.'

She swung back round to face him. 'Becky,' she said insistently.

'Mmm?' Jack nestled into the pillow, his eyes closed. 'You say something?'

She drew in a stiff breath. 'I don't like it when you call me Rebecca.'

He lifted his head off the pillow to look at her, his greener-than-green gaze meeting hers. 'It is your name, isn't it?'

'That's not the point,' she said. 'You only do it to annoy me. I know you do.'

He gave the pillow a soft thump and, settling back down, closed his eyes once more. 'You're imagining it. I have no intention of annoying you. I just don't like abbreviated names.'

'You abbreviate yours,' she pointed out. 'Jackson Colcannon is your full name.'

He opened one eye to look at her. 'I hate the name Jackson. It always reminds me of one or both of my parents being angry with me.'

'Now you know how I feel,' she said. 'No one ever called me by my full name unless they were cross with me, which means I can only assume from your persistence in calling me by it that you are always angry with me.' She gave him a probing look. '*Are* you angry with me?'

Jack wasn't sure how he should answer. Anger wasn't exactly the primary emotion he felt when around her, although it was certainly way up there. She made him feel edgy and uncomfortable at times, as if she could see things in him he didn't want her or anyone else to see. He assumed it was because she had known him so long, watching him reaching adulthood alongside her brother. But he wasn't really angry with her, or at least not right now. If anything, he was angry at himself. He had no business thinking about her in any other way than as a surrogate sister. And right now, with her soft pouting mouth and fluffy blonde hair, she didn't exactly look all that sisterly.

'Can we just go to sleep?' he asked, flinging a hand over his eyes.

Becky came over and pulled his hand away from his face. 'Not until you promise.'

He eased his hand out of the warm curl of her small fingers and stuffed it down by his side, not trusting himself not to tug her down on top of him on the sofa. He could already smell her perfume on the pillow under his head, the exotic fragrance filling his nostrils until he could barely think.

'Promise me, Jack,' she insisted, her breath brushing over his face.

His eyes met hers in the soft light of the lamplight.

'Becky, then.' His voice, to his annoyance, came out on a croak. 'There—I said it. Satisfied?'

Her soft mouth curved upwards in a smile. 'You see? That didn't hurt a bit, did it?'

He scowled at her as he thumped the pillow once more. 'Will you, please, go to bed and let me sleep in peace?'

''Night, Jack.' And on an impulse she couldn't stop in time, she bent down and pressed a soft, barely there kiss to his stubbly cheek, her silky blonde hair falling forward to caress his bare neck. 'Thanks for coming to my rescue tonight.'

He grunted something inaudible in response and covered his head with the pillow.

Jack listened to the soft pad of her bare feet as she made her way to her room, heard the rustle of the bedclothes as she slipped back into bed. After a few moments he heard the click of the bedside lamp going off and another soft rustle as she shifted in the bed to get more comfortable.

He gave a silent groan as his lower body sprang to life at the thought of her lying within a few feet of him, the pulse of blood thickening him almost painfully.

'Damn you, Rebecca Baxter,' he growled in a deep undertone.

'Did you say something, Jack?' Becky called out from her bedroom.

Jack gritted his teeth. 'Goodnight, Reb—Becky.'

After a few short moments he heard her bedclothes being

pushed aside, closely followed by the pad of her footsteps as she came back out to the sitting room.

'I just thought of something.' She shifted from one bare foot to another, her chocolate gaze a little reluctant to meet his. 'Were you…with someone tonight? I mean…you know, sleeping with someone?'

'Sleeping with someone?' He almost laughed out loud. The last time he'd slept with someone had been— Hell, had it been *that* long ago?

'I mean having sex with someone,' she said, her cheeks tinged with pink.

'I don't think I have to answer that question,' he said firmly. 'For a start it's none of your business, and secondly I—'

'It's not like I'm jealous or anything.' Becky quickly cut him off. 'I just thought it was highly presumptuous of me to assume you'd drop everything and come over here.' She inspected her hands for a moment. 'I didn't want there to be any trouble… I mean, you having to explain to a girlfriend that you'd spent the night with me.' She raised her eyes to his. 'I wouldn't want there to be any misunderstandings.'

'Trust me,' he said with a touch of wryness. 'There will be no misunderstandings. Apart from the police, no one knows I'm here.'

'You won't tell anyone at work, will you?' she asked after a little pause.

'Hell, no,' he said, laying his head back on the sofa.

She pursed her lips for a moment. 'You make it sound as if it's some sort of terrible punishment to spend the night with me.'

You're not wrong there, baby, he felt like saying, but didn't.

'You didn't have to stay,' she went on. 'I can look after myself.'

'Yeah, right, armed to the hilt with a pair of stilettos,' he muttered as he recalled her statement to the police. 'I'd be absolutely scared spitless if I encountered you in a dark alley.'

'You think you're so funny,' she bit out resentfully.

'I don't want to think anything right now except about how

many minutes I can shut my eyes before I have to open them again,' he said. 'Now, will you go back to bed or do I have to carry you?'

Becky did her best to hold his determined look, but in the end it was too much for her. She was overtired, overwrought and overcome with emotions she couldn't control any longer.

'I—I'm scared.' She waved a hand in the general direction of her bedroom. 'He was in there. I can still see him when I shut my eyes.'

Jack swore under his breath as he got off the sofa. He came across to where she was standing, putting his hands on the top of her slim shoulders, his eyes holding hers.

'I know I'm going to regret this, but do you want me to sleep in your bed with you just for tonight?' he asked.

'You'd *do* that?' she asked, her eyes wide with amazement. 'You mean you wouldn't mind?'

He gave her what he hoped was a carefree smile. 'It'll be a piece of cake,' he said. 'Which side do you want, right or left?'

She smiled up at him. 'Let's toss for it.'

CHAPTER THREE

JACK hadn't expected to get to sleep at all, so when he woke at sunrise to find Becky lying on her side, looking at him, it took him a moment or two to gather himself. Her shoulder-length blonde hair was all tousled, her full mouth soft and her pink satin pyjamas clinging to the curves of her body in all the right places.

'Did I snore?' he asked, trying not to stare at the tempting shadow between her breasts.

A small smile tugged at her mouth. 'No, but you do talk in your sleep.'

He stiffened. 'What did I say?'

She gave him a wouldn't-you-like-to-know wink and got out of bed. 'What would you like for breakfast?'

Jack swung his legs over his side of the bed and grimaced at the rumpled state of his trousers. 'I haven't got time for breakfast but can I borrow your iron?'

He left soon after his clothes were pressed, extracting a promise from her to get the locks changed before she came in to the hospital.

Becky watched him drive away and once his car had turned the corner she picked up the phone book and began to flip through the pages, looking for a twenty-four-hour locksmith.

Jack finished his round with the residents and entered the operating theatre where Gwen Taylor was setting up with two other nurses.

'Has Becky arrived yet?' he asked.

Gwen's eyebrows rose just a fraction at his use of Becky's preferred name.

'Becky is it now?' she mused. 'Wow, what brought that on?'

He gave her a quelling look. 'Can we bring in the first case now, Gwen? Time is getting on.'

'David Barker, the new orderly, has gone down to get her. Don't be so impatient, he's still learning the ropes,' Gwen said. With a twinkle in her eyes she added, 'You just do the surgery and I'll run the theatre.'

'Fine,' he said, 'but let's have none of that tea and scones routine this morning. I want these three cases done before lunch. Lately my lists seem to be turning into a list of meals interspersed with the occasional operation.'

'How very amusing you are this morning.' Gwen gave him a droll look. 'Here's the patient. Why don't you go and scrub while we get things organized?'

Jack rolled his eyes and shouldered open the scrub-room door. Gwen Taylor was a good scrub nurse but she had a tendency to try and matchmake, which irritated him intensely. If word got out that he'd spent the night at Becky's place, he'd never hear the end of it.

Becky watched as David, the orderly, and Susie, the anaesthetic nurse on duty, slid the patient from her bed to the operating table.

'Just feel the edge of the table, Mrs Oakland,' Susie said. 'It's pretty narrow. We don't want you to fall off so make sure you're settled in the middle.'

'It is narrow,' Mrs Oakland said as she settled herself. 'How's that?'

'Fine, that's perfect,' Susie said. 'I'm just going to cover you with a warm blanket while Dr Baxter puts in your IV line.'

Becky put a tourniquet on Mrs Oakland's arm, inserted an IV cannula and started the drip while Susie held an oxygen mask over the patient's nose and mouth, encouraging her to take big breaths.

'The mask smells a bit rubbery, Mrs Oakland,' Becky said, 'but this is just oxygen to make you nice and ready.' She began to inject propofol into the IV line. 'You'll start to feel a bit sleepy now; you'll just drift off to sleep.'

Betty Oakland murmured something about feeling light-headed but her words soon began to slur and she drifted off into unconsciousness.

'Size 6 reinforced tube, please, Susie, with the introducer in. Thanks. She has a very small larynx,' Becky said.

She put the laryngoscope into the patient's mouth and elevated the tongue, taking care not to chip the teeth as she inserted the endotracheal tube. She connected the patient to the anaesthetic machine and started the volatile agents just as Jack walked in from the scrub sink. He dried his hands on a sterile towel before donning his gown and double gloves.

'Right to prep, Dr Baxter?' he asked.

Becky caught the tail end of Gwen's speculative look.

'She's asleep, *Mr* Colcannon,' she said with a hard little glance his way. If he was going to go all formal on her then she would do the same to him.

'Can you give a gram of cephalosporin and 5000 units heparin?'

'Already done,' Becky said.

Jack prepped and draped the abdomen with the registrar's help, applying a steridrape and setting up the diathermy, positioning the scratch pad and sucker.

'What do you think the splenic mass is, Mr Colcannon?' Robert asked.

'My guess is lymphoma. The spleen is so large that it's causing pain and thrombocytopenia. That reminds me, Dr Baxter, we've got platelets available if we run into bleeding. I'll give you warning if we need to access them.'

'Right, I've checked myself and they've already been brought round to the blood fridge in case,' Becky said.

'Prepared for just about anything, aren't you, Dr Baxter?' His eyes met hers for a moment.

'I always try to be prepared,' she answered. 'I don't like nasty surprises.'

He held her challenging look for a single heartbeat before holding out his gloved hand towards Gwen. 'Scalpel.'

He made a long upper midline incision and completed the abdominal opening with diathermy.

'That's one hell of a spleen,' Robert observed.

'Yes, and adherent to the diaphragm, too,' Jack said. 'I'm going to have to take the vessels first. At least this is a controlled splenectomy, not like that last ruptured spleen that bled out a couple of litres.'

'What a night that was,' Robert recalled with a visible shudder.

'That's the splenic artery clamped now,' Jack said. 'The spleen should shrink a bit through the splenic vein. Let's start to mobilise it while that happens, then I'll take the vein.'

'She's oozy, Mr Colcannon,' Robert said. 'What about the platelets?'

'Yes, I agree. Can you give the five packs of platelets, Dr Baxter?'

Becky turned to Susie. 'Get the platelets now, please. We'll run them through a side line with the normal saline.'

Susie returned with the bags of platelets which she and Becky checked, then started to administer one by one, each over about ten minutes.

'The spleen is freeing up everywhere but the diaphragm, Robert,' Jack said. 'I'll take the splenic vein now then sharp dissect it off the diaphragm.' He clamped and divided and ligated the splenic vein, freeing the spleen from its vascular pedicle.

'She's getting a few ventricular ectopic beats, Jack, I'm not sure why,' Becky informed him, momentarily forgetting her determination to address him formally.

'I've just got to get the spleen off the diaphragm and then we're through,' he said. Taking long dissecting scissors, he started to free the spleen from the diaphragm. 'There's no plane between spleen and diaphragm, Robert.'

'I think there's a hole in the diaphragm,' Robert said.

'Yes, it's plastered to the spleen. Dr Baxter, I'm going to

have to create a diaphragmatic defect to get this spleen out. I'll repair in the end. How's the patient?'

'VEBs all over,' Becky said. 'PO2's OK, we can oxygenate her fine. I'm not worried about the diaphragm, but this dysrhythmia's worrying. Susie, set up a Xylocaine infusion and I'm taking bloods for electrolytes and cardiac isoenzymes. Maybe she's had a silent infarct, although the ECG trace looks OK.'

'Diaphragm's repaired,' Jack said after a few more minutes. 'We're putting in a suction drain to the splenic bed and we're out of here.'

'The sooner the better,' Becky said, watching the monitor closely. 'I want this patient in the cardiac unit and a cardiologist on board. Susie, can you get me Dr Lockney on the phone in Cardiology and tee up a bed with the coronary care unit?'

'Sure,' Susie said, picking up the phone.

Jack lifted out the massive spleen, inserted the drain and closed the abdomen. He stepped away from the table once he'd finished, while Robert and Gwen dressed the wound and attached the drain to the suction bottle.

Jack stripped off his gown and protective head gear as he left Theatre to write up his notes on the operation.

'What's next on the list?' Robert asked as he took off his gloves. 'Have we got time for a quick cup of coffee?'

Gwen shook her head. 'Jack is in one of his let's-work-right-through-no-breaks moods.' She flicked her gaze to Becky, who was reversing the anaesthetic on Mrs Oakland. 'What's with all this Dr Baxter stuff, Becky? I thought him calling you Rebecca was bad enough. Don't tell me you ran into his car again.'

'You know what Jack is like,' Becky said, trying her best not to colour up. 'He likes to keep his distance.'

'He must have a new lady in his life,' Susie said. 'One of the nurses on Surgical A told me she was trying to track him down about a patient's pain relief during the night and he didn't answer his land line or his mobile.'

'That's probably why he wants to speed things up around here,' Gwen said with a mischievous little smile. 'He's in a hurry to get home to offload some of those hormones of his.'

Becky was relieved she had to accompany the patient out to Recovery. She'd had one too many of Gwen's speculative looks cast her way and didn't want to encourage any more.

The rest of the morning's list passed without incident and although Jack maintained his cool formal distance, she'd caught him looking at her once or twice, a small frown settling between his dark brows. She imagined he was regretting his offer to stay over the previous night, silently dreading it leaking out into the hospital gossip network.

It wasn't as if she was under any illusions as to her supermodel potential, and she was the first to admit she didn't even come close to his ex's designer elegance, but did he have to make it so obvious he wasn't interested?

Although she knew it was petty of her, she couldn't help feeling a little disappointed he hadn't even tried to make a move on her while they'd shared her bed. Most men would have had a quick grope at the very least, but not Jack. He had kept his trousers on and his hands to himself all night.

She peered at herself in the female change-room mirror and grimaced. She had surgical-cap hair and not a scrap of make-up on, not even lip gloss.

She ran her hands over her hips and sighed. She hadn't been to the gym in months and it was starting to show, and with Christmas just around the corner she knew it could only get worse.

'Right, my girl.' She addressed her reflection with determination. 'You are going on a diet and exercise programme, effective immediately.'

Her car was hot from being parked in the sun all day but Becky refused to be daunted. She drove to her flat and, after cautiously checking each room, quickly changed into running gear, scooped up the new keys she'd had cut that morning and jogged outside into the golden light of the evening.

She was ashamed of how breathless she was after simply running to the corner of her street. Ben had been telling her for years how important it was to get and stay fit but she'd never made the time to do it properly. He'd even suggested self-defence classes but she'd laughed at him, telling him the only wrestling she wanted to do with a man was the type that led to marriage and kids.

She knew it was probably terribly old-fashioned of her but all she had really ever wanted was to settle down and bring up a family, the way her parents had done for her and Ben. In her hurry to achieve her dream, she had blundered into three disastrous relationships, each one ending sourly. It still made her cringe to think of how she'd acted so impulsively, hurting three quite decent men in the process.

It wasn't that she didn't love her career—she did, and had even chosen it for its practicality—but she still secretly longed for that once-in-a-lifetime connection with one special person. What was life about if not companionship and intimacy? She didn't want to spend the rest of her life putting people to sleep during the day and coming home to sleep alone at night. Last night had shown her that, if nothing else. Waking up next to Jack had been so special, even though he hadn't touched her.

She'd watched him for ages before he'd woken up, studying his features, wishing she'd had the courage to reach out and trace her fingers over the dark shadows under his eyes which always seemed to be there...

She stopped running and took several deep breaths as her thoughts caught up. What was she thinking? That Jack was that special person she'd been waiting for all her life?

No!

Not Jack Colcannon.

She choked back a laugh. She couldn't possibly fall in love with her brother's best friend. Ben would be appalled. Her parents would be...

No.

Jack wasn't marriage material. He was more the date-them-and-drop-them type. She couldn't imagine him allowing himself to feel anything but disdain for her. He couldn't even bring himself to call her by her preferred name.

Besides, he was practically an honorary brother. He'd seen her with braces and break-outs on her skin, for heaven's sake!

Except there was that one time twelve years ago, when he hadn't acted quite like a brother...

'I haven't got time to take you for a driving lesson,' Ben had said. 'Ask Jack. He won't mind.'

Becky had pouted at her brother. 'Jack is a guest, I can't ask him.'

'Jack is practically a member of our family. He's been here for the last four weekends in a row. Surely you don't have to be shy around him now.'

'I'm not shy!'

Ben had given an amused chuckle as he'd spread out the weekend paper. 'No, that you're not. Go on, get out of here, brat, and ask him to teach you to reverse park. I'm resigning.'

She'd swung away in resentment. How like her brother to remind her of her failure to grasp the basic skills of reverse parking. So, she'd run into a few cars. So what? How else was she going to learn how to do it?

'Jack?' She found him under the shade of one of the elm trees in the garden, reading a medical journal. 'Can I ask you something?'

Jack put the journal down and lifted his head, his green eyes meeting hers. 'Sure, Rebecca. What's on your mind?'

She shifted from foot to foot like the awkward schoolgirl she was. Something about Jack always made her feel a bit self-conscious. She knew his father was a cosmetic surgeon and she couldn't help wondering if Jack thought she could do with some work herself. A little liposuction wouldn't go astray, and as for her breasts, which had been a bit slow on the uptake...

'I was wondering if you'd take me for a driving lesson,' she said. 'Ben has given up on me and my test is next month and—'

He got to his feet, his tall lean body casting a shadow over her five-foot-five frame.

'I guess I've got nothing better to do,' he said.

'Thanks,' she said, and added under her breath, 'I think.'

'Which car?'

'Can we take yours?' she asked, suddenly beaming up at him. 'I think I need to practise on a manual. Mum's is automatic and it's just not the same.'

She followed him out to where his car was parked and, after positioning her learner plates on the rear and front of the car, slipped behind the wheel.

'Wow,' she said, running her hands over the shiny dashboard. 'This is so cool. A real sports car!'

'Where do you want to drive to?' Jack asked.

She swivelled in her seat to face him. 'I would *love* to drive past Amelia Brockhurst's place out on the Ridgeway road. She'll be green with envy when she sees me driving this.'

A few bunny-hopping minutes later Becky felt as if she'd more or less got the hang of the gears and drove with increasing confidence out towards the Ridgeway road.

'Driving in a straight line is no real test of your ability,' Jack said. 'You need to practise some of the manoeuvres the examiner will be looking out for, like parking and hill starts.'

'OK,' she said, 'I'll do a hill start on the next hill we come to.'

Within a few minutes they came to an intersection with a stop sign and a steep incline.

'Will this do?' she asked, swinging a glance his way.

'Show me your stuff,' he said, bracing himself.

The car coughed and jerked as she let out the clutch, but somehow she managed to get over the hill without stalling, although there was a slight smell of burning clutch-plate lingering in the air.

'Hey! Am I good or what?' she crowed delightedly. 'Wait till I tell Ben. He thinks I'm hopeless at hill starts.'

'Let's do a reverse park,' Jack suggested. 'Drive on a bit until we come to somewhere suitable.'

'Somewhere suitable' turned out to be an old quarry where some forty-four-gallon drums had been left abandoned. Jack got out of the car to position them the approximate distance so she could practise.

'Turn the wheel now,' he directed, but she hit the drum regardless.

'I can't do it!'

'Yes, you can,' he said, getting back into the passenger seat, making an obvious effort not to notice the scratch on his paintwork. 'Now, try once more. Put your indicator on and swing the wheel to the right.'

She did as he instructed and managed to position the car without touching the drum.

'Did I pass?' She looked at him hopefully.

'Not until you do it on the other side,' he said.

'The other side?' She gaped at him. 'But I can't do it on the other side!'

'You have to be able to do it on both sides,' he said. 'What about one-way streets? You have to prove you can do it no matter what direction the traffic flows.'

She bit her lip in concentration and started to reverse, but the drum connected with the bumper bar and toppled over.

'Oops!'

'Try it again,' Jack said.

She tried it again but this time she almost flattened the drum. She bent her head to the steering-wheel and groaned in despair. 'I'm going to fail. I just know I am.'

'No, you're not,' Jack said, touching her on the shoulder to bring her gaze back to his. 'You can do this. I know you can.'

Becky could feel the warmth of his long fingers through the thin cotton of her top. Her eyes flicked to his mouth, her tongue snaking out to moisten her lips.

'Do you really think I can do it?' she whispered into the air that separated them.

'Yes. Now, try it again,' he said, letting his hand fall away.

'Run alongside the drum as if it is a parked car and now swing your wheels to—'

Crunch.

'You're not concentrating, Rebecca,' Jack said, gritting his teeth.

'I *am* concentrating!' she flashed back in frustration.

'No, you're not,' he said. 'You're going at it like a bull at a gate. Take your time and—'

Becky flung open the driver's door and slammed it behind her, stomping off in a temper fuelled by repeated failure and embarrassment.

'Rebecca.' He got out of the car to stride after her.

'Don't call me that!' She swung back to face him. 'No one but you ever calls me that.'

He set his jaw and eyeballed her determinedly, his hands tightly clenched at his sides.

'Get back in the car and try it again.'

'No.' She folded her arms across her chest, glaring back at him with spirited defiance. 'You can't make me.'

Two beats of silence passed.

'You think not?' he said, reaching for her, and pulled her towards him ruthlessly.

She stared at the grim line of his mouth for a moment, her stomach hollowing out at the determined glitter in his gaze as it collided with hers.

'*Get in the damn car,*' he ordered, his fingers tightening on her upper arms.

She lifted her chin, her chocolate brown eyes issuing an irresistible challenge. 'Make me.'

Becky brought herself back to the present with a jolt. She didn't want to recall that bruising kiss that had led to the stiff unbroken silence as Jack had driven them back to her parents' property. She didn't want to remember how his mouth had felt against the softness of hers, how her body had pressed itself against the solid hardness of his as if looking for a lifetime anchor.

She ran all the way back to her flat, gasping for breath as

if all the hounds of hell and purgatory and the council dogs' home were after her, coming to an abrupt halt as she came to the door of her flat.

It was swinging open.

CHAPTER FOUR

BECKY sucked in a breath and stared at the open door for a few moments, weighing up her options. She could call the police but her mobile was on her bed where she'd flung it earlier in her hurry to get changed. The landline was within reach but she wasn't sure she wanted to enter her flat if there was an unknown assailant inside.

'Hello?' she called out in a somewhat forced light breezy tone, as if expecting a long-lost friend to greet her. 'I'm home!'

She pushed the door open a little further, her eyes widening in shock at the disarray of her flat. Books and papers were scattered and most of the furniture overturned, as if someone had been intent on searching through her possessions for something important.

She stepped over the mess and moved through to the bedroom. She bent to pick up one of her dresses off the floor, a lightning bolt of alarm rocketing through her as she looked at the slash that had rent it in two.

Her eyes went to the mirrored doors of the built-in wardrobe, her heart coming to a complete standstill when she saw what was scrawled across it in one of her blood-red lipsticks.
GET OUT OR DIE BITCH FACE

Becky allowed herself one small swallow, doing her best to keep her head, as icy fear crawled like a long-legged insect right up her spine to settle amongst the fine hairs on the back of her neck, lifting each one in turn.

She reached blindly for the phone and dialled the emergency code.

'Colcannon,' Jack answered his mobile as he ran the last block back to his house near Bondi Beach.

'Jack, it's me, Ben.'

Jack stopped running. 'Hey, mate, long time no hear. How are you go—?'

'Listen to me, Jack.' Ben cut him off, his voice low and urgent. 'I can't talk for long, this call might be traced. I'm in trouble.'

'What sort of trouble?' Jack frowned.

'I can't tell you all the details,' Ben said. 'I'm on a big undercover assignment. The biggest of my career. But some-one is trying to flush me out.'

'Who?'

'Someone on the inside of the operation is acting as an informant.' He took a ragged breath and continued, 'I can't let this operation slip. It's at a crucial stage. It'll be the biggest criminal bust we've had in years. It's vital my identity isn't revealed.' He paused for a moment and added, 'I need your help.'

'Anything, Ben,' Jack said. 'What do you want me to do?'

'I need you to look after Becky. She's in danger. Big dan-ger.'

Jack felt a chill pass through his body and for some reason he couldn't get his voice to work immediately.

'They know her brother is in the ring, but they don't know which one of us it is. There are a couple of us working un-dercover. They're trying to flush me out by targeting her. It'll blow the operation if I break my cover now. That's what they want.'

'They?' Jack finally managed to croak.

'It's a drug operation,' Ben said. 'They know someone has infiltrated them but they're not sure who it is. This is like a process of elimination. A few buttons are getting pressed to see who responds.'

Jack wondered if he should tell Ben about Becky's intruder the night before, but decided against it. His friend sounded stressed enough as it was, without him adding to it.

'You've got to keep an eye on Becky for me,' Ben said. 'I need to know she's safe at all times.'

'What about the police?' Jack suggested. 'If you're so worried, shouldn't she have some sort of official protection?'

'*No!*' Ben's tone was insistent. 'We can't involve the regular force. We have to handle this by ourselves. You're the only one I trust, Jack. I think someone on the force is feeding this informant. I'm not prepared to take any risks.'

'You're starting to really scare me, mate,' Jack confessed.

'I'm sorry to involve you, Jack.' Ben's tone was hollow with anguish. 'But you are the only person I know I can trust and who's in a position to protect Becky.'

'I'm not sure I'm the right person for the job,' Jack said after a small but telling silence. 'Becky and I don't always see eye to—'

'If they have to kill her to get to me, they won't think twice about it,' Ben interjected bluntly. 'My parents are overseas and hard to trace, but Becky is a sitting duck. You've got to get her out of that flat, Jack. I don't care how you do it, even if you have to pretend to be in love with her to get her to come and live with you. You can explain it all to her later, but for now the word out on the loop has hinted if she stays in that building another night she'll be in the morgue by morning.'

Jack felt his stomach give a sudden lurch and was surprised his voice came out at all, let alone calmly. 'Should I tell her she's in danger?'

'No…don't do that,' Ben said after a short pause. 'If she knows it's to do with me, she might do something to lead them to me, something stupid. Just stick like glue to her outside work hours. That's what a man in love does, right?'

'She'll never fall for it,' Jack warned him. 'How am I going to convince her to spend time with me when we've been at each other's throats for years?'

'I'm sure you'll think of something,' Ben said. 'You'll have to. I don't think anyone will try anything inside the hospital—they probably wouldn't get back out past Security if they did. But after hours…' He let his trailed-off sentence say the rest for him.

'I'll do what I can,' Jack promised.

'Thanks, mate,' Ben said. 'I knew I could call on you. Just don't let anything happen to her. She's my kid sister and I love her, brat that she is.'

'How can I contact you?'

'You can't,' Ben said. 'I'm taking a risk now in calling you.'

There was a small silence before Ben added, his voice rough with bitten-back emotion, 'Jack…if anything was to happen to me…you'll tell my folks I love them, won't you?'

'Yes, of course, Ben, of course I would.' Jack swallowed the restriction in his throat.

'If I don't come out of this, don't let Becky throw herself away on some creep,' Ben added. 'She has terrible taste in men. I don't want to see her get hurt.'

'I'll do my best but—'

Ben broke off the connection without saying goodbye, which Jack somehow knew had been deliberate.

He stared at the mobile in his hands for some time, wondering if he'd just imagined the conversation he'd had with his best mate. He knew Ben's work was dangerous—every cop lived with the threat of death hanging over them in the line of duty—but this time his friend sounded as if he was in well and truly over his head.

The phone began to ring in his hand and he almost dropped it in surprise, his fingers fumbling to answer it.

'Colcannon.'

'Jack. It's me, Becky.'

Jack's hand tightened on the phone. 'Becky, are you—?' He stopped in mid-sentence, recalling Ben's insistence she wasn't to be informed of the danger she was in. 'I mean, how are you?'

'I've been robbed,' she said. 'The police are here and—'

'*The police!*'

Becky frowned at his tone. 'Yes, they're still here taking photos and so on.'

'I'll be right over,' he said. 'Don't go anywhere until I get there.'

'But I'm on call at the hospital,' she said. 'I have to go in right now. I had a call a few minutes ago. I have to assess a patient in A and E.'

'Right…' Jack forced his brain into gear. Ben had said he thought she would be fairly safe at the hospital so maybe that was the best place for her right now. 'I'll meet you there in a few minutes.'

'But you're not on call tonight, Brendan Fairbrother is.'

'I'm covering for him from nine this evening,' he lied.

'That's funny, he didn't mention it to me and I was just talking to him.'

'It was arranged weeks ago,' he said, privately amazed at how easy lying was once you got used to it. 'I'll ring him and remind him. It's his anniversary, he's probably forgotten. See you soon.'

Becky didn't get a chance to respond as he cut off the call. She turned to the police officers who were just finishing up their crime scene investigation, wondering how in the world her life had suddenly become so frighteningly complicated.

'Dr Baxter,' Constable Daniels addressed her solemnly. 'It might be a good idea if you stayed off the premises for a few days until we catch this guy. This doesn't look like a prank. Until we know for sure, it might be best to stay somewhere else, preferably with someone with whom you feel safe.' He handed her a card with his name and contact numbers on it. 'Call me at any time if you think of anything else that might help us in our investigation.'

She nodded in agreement, tucking the card away as she picked up a few items of clothing that hadn't been slashed, wondering who amongst her friends she could ask to use a spare bedroom for a few days.

If only she could contact Ben! He was the one and only person who made her feel safe.

Well…maybe not the only person…

* * *

Not long after she'd done an anaesthetic preassessment on a nineteen-year-old girl with acute appendicitis, Becky received a call from A and E informing her that a motorbike accident victim was on his way. As part of the trauma team she was required in A and E to manage IV and airway for trauma cases.

She ran into Jack on her way through to the resus room, where the ambulance officers were transferring the patient on a spine board from the ambulance trolley to the resus bed.

She began her assessment as Jack got a rapid history from the ambulance officers.

'We picked him up half an hour ago, Mr Colcannon. He'd been on a high-powered motorbike and impacted with a steel pylon holding a guard rail, obviously at high speed.'

'What was his GCS at the scene?' Jack asked.

'Unresponsive to anything,' the ambulance officer informed him. 'Totally unconscious. We extracted his helmet and stabilised his neck with a hard collar, got in an IV line and bagged and masked him to here.'

'Good work, guys,' Jack said. 'We'll resuscitate him and then I'll catch up with you before you go for any other details.'

Becky looked up as Jack approached the patient.

'I've intubated him, Jack. He's deeply unconscious and has a difficult airway to maintain. He didn't need any drugs. I just put the endotracheal tube down.'

'Primary survey first,' Jack said. 'Airway is secured.' He listened with a stethoscope before percussing the patient's chest. 'Resonant on both sides and good air entry. No visible chest injury. Pulse and BP?'

'Pulse 120, BP 80 systolic,' the nurse on duty informed him.

'Get in IV lines, Dr Baxter, and start colloid and O-negative blood fast, and get some blood off for cross-match, haemoglobin, electrolytes and amylase.' He examined the patient's abdomen by inspection first, then palpation and percussion, and after that listened with his stethoscope.

'Abrasions and bruising extensively over the left flank and a large haematoma. His abdo's distended and tense, dull to percussion and no bowel sounds. He's clearly got major intra-abdominal bleeding.' He turned to the nurse. 'Can you put in a urinary catheter and nasogastric tube? Dr Baxter, how are those drips going?'

'Both in and running full bore,' Becky said. 'He's getting hard to ventilate, his abdomen looks distended and is compressing his diaphragm.'

'Shall I get CT organised so we can see where his bleeding's coming from?' Robert asked.

'There's no way this guy's going to CT. He's in hypovolaemic shock, class 3 at least, we're barely keeping up, and his ventilation's going off because of intra-abdominal tension. He doesn't need a CT, he needs surgery, and now. Get the emergency theatre on line right away. Dr Baxter, are you right to get him to Theatre now?'

'The sooner the better, Jack,' Becky said. 'We need that abdomen opened and decompressed so I can ventilate him.'

'Good, get the orderlies in now, and you go up with him in the lift. Keep that O-negative blood going in fast while I get up to Theatre and scrub.'

The orderlies wheeled the trolley into the emergency lift from A and E straight up to the theatre complex, with Becky and Robert continuing resuscitation on the way.

Jack was already scrubbed with the theatre team by the time the patient was wheeled through the emergency theatre door. The patient was slid onto the operating table and Jack prepped and draped the abdomen rapidly.

'Don't worry about a steridrape, Sandra,' he said to the emergency scrub nurse. 'And I want two sump suckers on board and diathermy up to 50 coag. Robert, get scrubbed and in here and call the intern—we need an extra pair of hands.'

As Robert gowned and gloved, Jack made a long midline abdominal incision. A huge fountain of dark blood gushed from the wound over the side of the abdomen and onto the floor.

'Suck, Robert, with both suckers. Packs, Sandra.'

Jack scooped out three litres of blood and clot from the abdomen and identified the source of bleeding.

'Give me a long artery forceps. Pull hard on that retractor, Robert, I've got to see the splenic pedicle.' He applied a nine-inch artery forceps to the splenic artery and vein, then individually clamped the artery and vein and lifted out the spleen.

'Heavy catgut, Sandra,' he instructed. 'Full length, don't cut it, I've got to tie down deep.' He tied off the splenic artery and then tied off and oversewed the splenic vein.

'Looks like we haven't damaged the pancreatic tail in those ties, and stomach looks OK. One of the short gastrics is still bleeding.' Jack tied off the remaining bleeders and then carried out a thorough laparotomy to exclude any other intra-abdominal injury. Confident there was none and after sucking out any residual blood he closed the abdomen.

'That was amazing, Mr Colcannon,' Sandra said. 'I have never seen so much blood before.' She looked down at the floor and added, 'Or so well controlled.'

Jack grunted something in response and turned away to strip off his gown and gloves, catching Becky's look on the way past.

'She's right, Jack,' Becky said. 'We were sailing pretty close to the wind but you pulled it off.'

He gave a little shrug as he shouldered open the door. 'I'm sure Brendan would have handled it just as well.'

The door swung shut behind him and Becky looked down at the still unconscious patient. Brendan Fairbrother was a competent enough surgeon, but he wasn't as skilled at handling trauma as Jack was. In fact, there were few surgeons at St Patrick's who could match him for a cool head under pressure.

'He's one hell of a surgeon, isn't he?' Sandra said as she stripped off her gloves, sidestepping the massive pool of blood on the floor.

'He certainly is,' Robert agreed. 'But I thought Brendan Fairbrother was on call this evening. Did they do a last-minute swap?'

'It's Brendan's anniversary,' Becky said as she and the an-aesthetic nurse began to transfer the patient to recovery.

'Anniversary?' Robert looked at Sandra. 'I didn't even know Mr Fairbrother was married.'

Sandra waited until Becky had left Theatre before respond-ing, 'He's not married and as far as I know he hasn't got any anniversaries to celebrate.'

'So what gives?'

Sandra gave him a speculative little smile. 'I think our Mr Colcannon is developing rather a soft spot for Becky Baxter.'

'No way!' Robert said disbelievingly. 'He hardly even looks her in the eye.'

'You need to be a little more astute, my boy,' Sandra said, poking a playful finger at his chest. 'That man is on a mission, you mark my words.'

'What sort of mission?'

'He wants to be with her as often as he can,' she said. 'Why else would he offer to be on call two nights in a row?'

Robert rolled his lips for a moment. 'Maybe you're right. Who wants to be on call two nights in a row?'

Sandra gave him a knowing wink. 'Who indeed?'

Becky did her best to settle the young appendicectomy patient who was nervous about having her very first general anaes-thetic.

'You won't remember a thing,' she assured her. 'As soon as I inject the drug into your IV line you'll start to feel sleepy. Next thing you'll be in Recovery and feeling a bit sore but it will all be over.'

'Will it hurt?'

'You'll be a bit uncomfortable for a few days after surgery but nothing a couple of painkillers can't handle. You'll be back out partying before you know it.'

'I'm missing three parties as it is,' Emma Stockport said, wincing as Becky found a vein.

'You and me, too,' Becky said with a smile. 'The lead-up to Christmas is a bit full on, isn't it?'

'Tell me about it,' Emma said, looking at the cannula Becky had inserted into the back of her hand. 'Eeuuw, that looks totally gross.'

'Start counting, Emma,' Becky said, feeding the propofol into her line.

'One…two….thr…'

Jack came in scrubbed and took a sterile towel off the trolley to dry his hands before putting on his gown and gloves.

'This will be a cinch after the last case,' he said, addressing Robert who had gowned alongside him. 'Want me to talk you through it?'

'Thanks, yes, that would be good. My logbook's looking pretty bare at the moment. None of the other consultants seem to have time to take me through cases.'

'Well, now's the time. Robert, start prepping and drape the patient.'

Robert prepped the abdomen with Betadine and draped the right iliac fossa with green drapes.

'Make your incision in the skin crease two thirds the way out along a line from the umbilicus to the anterior superior iliac spine. About 5 centimetres long,' Jack coached as Sandra handed Robert the scalpel in a yellow kidney dish.

Jack talked Robert gently through each step of the procedure, correcting Robert's technical uncertainties and guiding him to complete an uncomplicated appendicectomy.

'Good work. Close the skin with a subcuticular vicryl. Make sure she gets a stat dose of cephalosporin as wound infection prophylaxis. You can write up the op notes, and put yourself down as the primary surgeon and me as the assistant.'

'Thanks, Mr Colcannon, that was great,' Robert said with a grateful smile.

Becky was just coming out of the change room when Jack stepped forward from where he'd been leaning against the wall of the corridor, seemingly waiting for her to appear.

'I'm just on my way home,' he said. 'I was wondering if you wanted to grab a bite to eat somewhere.'

Becky stared at him blankly for a few seconds without responding. Jack ran a hand through the dark silk of his hair and shifted his gaze a fraction to the left of hers.

'I've been thinking about your flat,' he said. 'You probably don't want to stay there right now.' He glanced up and down the corridor before adding, 'I have a spare bedroom you could use for as long as you need to.'

Becky wasn't sure why he was issuing the invitation. His body language was giving off totally confusing signals. He looked distinctly uncomfortable, as if he was only offering out of a sense of duty.

'I wouldn't want to inconvenience you in any way,' she said crisply, making her way past him to the front exit.

'Hey.' He caught one of her arms on the way past and turned her around to face him. 'It's not an inconvenience. Really.'

She locked eyes with his. 'What's all this about, Jack?'

He let her arm go, his expression instantly guarded. 'What's all what about?'

She gave him one of her you-can't-fool-me looks. 'Come on, Jack, back in Theatre it was ''Dr Baxter'' this and ''Dr Baxter'' that, now you're offering me room and board. What's going on?'

His eyes fell away from hers. 'You've had back-to-back scares with an intruder and a robbery. I thought you might like some company for a few days until things settle down a bit.'

'Maybe you should define exactly what you mean by ''company'',' she said. 'You can barely be polite to me at work—how much worse would it be at your house?'

'Look, I know I haven't been all that friendly towards you, but I have my reasons.'

She rolled her eyes and swung away to the exit. 'Please, spare me your stupid reasons. Do you think I give a termite's toenail if you can't even get my name past the hard line of your lips?' She pressed the night button to release the front door and glared back at him over her shoulder. 'I'll book into a hotel until I get my place sorted out. Thanks for the offer but, no, thanks. I can look after myself.'

She was quite proud of her exit line, it suggested confidence and an assurance that she was still in control of her life no matter what red herrings were dished up to her. It was only when she got to her car at the far end of the hospital car park that she realised her confidence was really all a sham. She stared down at the shredded tyres on her car, and the cold long-legged insect of fear returned to tiptoe its way back up her spine.

Jack came to stand beside her, looking down at the viciously slashed rubber, his expression grim.

'Jack?' she whispered, blindly reaching for his hand, curling her small fingers around its solid warmth.

He squeezed her hand.

Just once. Briefly.

But it was enough.

'Let's go home to my place,' he said, and led her towards his car.

CHAPTER FIVE

BECKY sat in the passenger seat of Jack's car in silence. Fear had leaked into every layer of her skin until she felt as if she could even smell it. Her palms were sticky, her heart tripping erratically, her bent knees in front of her finding it hard to keep from knocking against each other.

'I wish I could talk to Ben.' She tied and untied her hands in her lap in agitation. 'He'd know what to do.'

'He'd want you to do what you're doing right now,' Jack assured her. 'To stay with me until the dust settles. I'll have your car delivered to the mechanic tomorrow. In the meantime, you can travel to work with me.'

'Who is doing this?' She swivelled in her seat to look at him. 'Who can possibly be doing this, and why?'

He stared straight ahead at the traffic lights while he waited for them to change to green. 'I wouldn't take any of this too personally. People get robbed all the time.'

'Are you for real?' Becky stared at him incredulously. 'I wasn't just robbed! I had a man in my bedroom, shining a torch in my face, for God's sake! Now my tyres have been slashed…' She stopped and gave one quick convulsive swallow. 'The three flat tyres.' Her eyes were wide with increasing fear.

'People get flat tyres all the time,' he said.

'That wasn't what you were saying the other day,' she pointed out, resentment creeping into her tone. 'You thought I was making it up.'

'All right, so I was wrong.' He sent her a quick unreadable glance. 'Anyway, you're nearly always late for work. You know how it gets on my nerves when I can't start my lists on time.'

'Well, bully for you, Mr Punctual,' she bit back. 'But, unlike you, other people have a life that occasionally gets in the way of being at work a whole hour before they need to.'

'I do not get to work an hour before I need to.'

'Yes, you do. You're always there early, champing at the bit, biting everyone's head off.'

'You make me sound like a complete tyrant,' he said. 'I just want to get the job done. I hate wasting time, and sometimes the under-funded public system can be frustrating.'

'Then why stay? Why not move over to the private sector and make a mint instead of the house-staff wage you're currently on?'

'I have my reasons.'

'Oh, yes.' Her tone was deliberately scathing. 'Those little reasons of yours.'

'Look, Rebecca…' his fingers tightened around the steering-wheel '…I have more than enough money. Besides, someone has to do something about the waiting lists. If every specialist bails out of the public hospital, the uninsured public they cut their teeth on in training will be left abandoned. Someone has to stick in there and solve the problems, not walk away.'

'If you call me Rebecca or Dr Baxter once more, I'll scream.'

'Oh, for God's sake,' he muttered as he turned into his street.

'I mean it, Jack.' She faced him determinedly. 'Do it one more time and your ears will suffer. Don't say I didn't warn you.'

He stabbed the remote control and drove into his garage, his jaw tight with frustration. *So help me, God, I'll kill you myself, Ben, for getting me into this,* he thought as he wrenched on the handbrake.

Becky followed him into his house, looking around with undisguised interest. It wasn't quite the 'Home of the Year' showcase mansion his father and current stepmother resided in, neither was it the comfortable, rambling family homestead where she and her brother had spent their childhood, but for all that it was spacious, if a little formally decorated for her taste.

'There are three spare rooms,' he informed her. 'You choose which one you'd prefer.'

Becky decided right then and there to choose the one closest his room just to annoy him.

'Why don't you give me a little tour?' she suggested.

He gave a grudging nod and showed her through the house, hurrying through it as if he couldn't wait to get away from her. Becky deliberately asked questions to prolong his agony.

'What's this cupboard for?'

'It's the linen cupboard,' he said, gritting his teeth. 'See?'

She peered inside and gave an inward smile at the neat piles of folded sheets and colour-coordinated towels. So, Mr Punctual was super-tidy as well.

'And which is your room?'

'That one there.'

'Where?'

'There.' He pointed vaguely to a room down the hall.

'Show me.'

'Whatever for?'

She folded her arms across her chest and tilted her head at him. 'Because I want to know the *real* you. I read this book once which said the way to truly know a person's personality is to meet their family of origin, go for a drive with them in their car and take a peek inside their bedroom.'

'I can't believe this,' he muttered. Striding down the hall, he opened the door for her. 'There. Analyse this.'

Becky inspected the neatly made bed, the spotless wall of mirrors on the inbuilt wardrobes, the neatly placed book by the bedside with a bookmark inside it instead of a dog-ear. Not a thing out of place and everything in its place.

'I knew it! You have obsessive-compulsive disorder,' she said, turning back to look up at him. 'I bet you wash your hands a hundred times a day, too.'

His green eyes went heavenwards in search of renewed patience. 'Of course I wash my hands a lot. I'm a surgeon, for heaven's sake.'

'You have issues of control.'

'Oh, for—'

'And you don't like disruption to your routine,' she said. 'It really gets under your skin. That's why this is really hard for you having me here, isn't it?'

You don't know the half of it, he thought with an inward grimace.

'I don't mind you being here,' he lied.

'What will we tell everyone at work?'

'Nothing,' he said. 'No one needs to know.'

'I'll have to let the hospital switchboard know,' she said. 'Otherwise how will they contact me when I'm on call?'

The line of his mouth tightened even further. 'Tell them you'll be only contactable on your mobile until further notice.'

'You see?' She gave him a triumphant look. 'You *are* uncomfortable with me being here. You don't want anyone to know about it. If you were at ease with it, you wouldn't give a damn who knew.'

'Listen, if my mother finds out you're staying here she'll have invitations in the mail by morning,' he said dryly.

'Invitations?' She looked up at him in confusion. 'Invitations for what?'

He gave her a grim look. 'Our wedding.'

'Oh.'

'"Oh" is right.' He rubbed his unshaven jaw. 'Come to think of it, if your parents hear about this…'

'They won't hear it from me,' she said.

'What if they ring you at your flat? Won't they worry when you don't answer?'

'They usually call or text me on my mobile, or send me emails, which I can access here or at work. Anyway, I can access my landline phone messages from off site.'

He gave a sudden frown. 'What about your clothes?' He glanced at his watch. 'I know it's late but perhaps we should go to your flat and get them.'

It was Becky's turn for displaying the grim look. 'The only clothes I have that are decent are the ones I'm wearing now. The rest have been hacked to pieces.'

'Oh.'

'I need to do some urgent shopping, but in the meantime do you have a T-shirt I could borrow to sleep in?'

He went to his wardrobe and pulled back one of the mirrored doors.

Becky peered around his shoulder, making *tsk tsk tsk* sounds in her throat.

'What?' He swung around to look at her.

She shook her head at him in mock despair. 'You are really anal.'

'Here.' He thrust an ironed and neatly folded T-shirt at her chest. 'And will you quit it with the character analysis? You're really starting to annoy me.'

She gave him a teasing smile. 'You are *so* uptight, Jack. You need to chill out a bit. You're acting like someone who was potty trained with a stun gun.'

'You know something, Rebecca, you are one of the most irritat—'

'Aaarrgghh!' Becky screamed at the top of her lungs, even going as far as plugging her own ears to escape the shrill, teeth-jarring sound.

'*Shut the hell up!*' Jack grasped her by the upper arms and gave her a little shake. 'Shut up! The neighbours will hear you!'

'I told you not to call me that. I warned you.' She took a big breath and squeezed her eyes shut. 'Aaarrgghh!'

'Damn it! If you don't shut up I'll do something we'll both end up regretting.'

Becky drew in another quick breath and opened her mouth for another good bellow, but before she could get the sound out Jack's mouth came down on hers and blocked off all sound except for the one tiny whimper that escaped from her lips before she could stop it. His mouth was hard and insistent, determined and ruthless in its mission to stop her from screaming.

As silencing methods went, it certainly worked, since she was so shocked she didn't even put up a fight. She felt herself weaken in his tight hold as his mouth changed its pressure, her stomach giving an unexpected somersault as his tongue flicked against hers, the heat and probe of it demanding a response from her she was in no way able to hold back. His tongue mated with hers, curling around hers intimately, the dart and retreat action stirring deep longings in her that she could feel reverberating in his hard body where it was pressed so insistently against hers.

Searing heat coursed through her from hips to breasts. She was aflame with a need she hadn't known she'd felt until his mouth had connected with hers. Her whole body was on fire, flames licking along her flesh until she thought she was going to explode with the sheer force of it.

His hands left her arms to grasp her head, angling it for better access, his long fingers buried in her hair, his lower body grinding into hers.

She felt every hard ridge as if they were standing together naked, the heat of his growing erection burning a pathway to her soul, melting her from the inside out. She could feel her body preparing itself, the liquid silk of desire swamping her, the delicate but intoxicating scent of mutual arousal rising upwards to tantalise and tempt.

She felt the sweep and plunge of his tongue, felt too the rasp of his unshaven jaw as he plundered her mouth even further, the scrape of masculine flesh on hers a delicious reminder of all that set them apart as man and woman.

Jack dragged his mouth off hers and stared down at her, his green eyes glazed with a combination of unrelieved desire and blistering anger.

Becky was the first to find her voice. 'You really shouldn't have done that,' she said.

A tiny nerve pulsed at the side of his mouth as he held her reproving look. 'You asked for it.'

Her brown eyes defied him. 'You called me Rebecca.'

He stepped away from her as if she'd burnt him.

'I must say, you've improved on your technique,' she added when he didn't respond. She ran a finger tip experimentally over her swollen lips. 'Only marginally, of course, but probably worth noting.'

He swung back to glare at her. 'You are the most annoying woman I've ever met, do you know that?'

She lifted her chin. 'Why? Because I won't let you walk all over me? That's your beef, isn't it, Jack? You can't control me. You can't put me in one of your neat little boxes like your stupid towels or T-shirts.'

'I don't know what you're talking about.'

'Yes, you do,' she insisted, coming up close to invade his personal space, pressing a finger to his chest. 'You hate the fact that I see through your keep-away-from-me mask. You've been doing it for years. You don't want anyone to get too close in case you start to feel something for them you just won't allow yourself to feel.'

'I don't feel anything for you.'

She gave him a narrow-eyed look. 'Then why did you just kiss me?'

'I wanted to shut you up.'

'You could have gagged me.'

His green eyes went to slits as he looked down at her. 'I could have strangled you too, but unfortunately there's a law against it.'

'Do you want to know what I think?' she asked.

'No. I do not want to know what you think. But no doubt you're going to tell me anyway.' His tone positively dripped with sarcasm.

Her mouth tilted in a knowing little smile. 'I think you wanted to kiss me.'

He didn't answer, but she could see that tiny, almost imperceptible pulse still leaping at the side of his set mouth, which indicated he wasn't as in control of his emotions as he would have liked.

For some reason Becky felt a tickle of excitement run over her for cracking his normally iron-clad control. She enjoyed teasing him, pushing him to the edge. She'd been doing it for years, although she wasn't entirely sure why.

'You wanted to kiss me, Jack, just like you did twelve years ago.'

'You were a spoilt brat twelve years ago,' he bit out. 'I shouldn't have kissed you then either, but it was either that or shake you till your teeth fell out.'

'Well, since you dislike me so much, I think it might be best if I call a taxi and go to the nearest hotel,' she said, picking her handbag up from the floor and taking out her mobile phone.

'*No!*' He snatched the phone out of her hand and held it out of reach.

Becky's eyebrows rose in twin arches. 'You know, Jack, along with strangling, holding someone against their will is also against the law.'

'I want you to stay with me,' he said from between clenched teeth.

'Why?'

'It's three a.m. I don't like the idea of you trawling the city for a hotel at this hour.'

'How terribly chivalrous of you but, really, I'm a big girl now and can quite easily find myself somewhere to stay.' She made a grab for her phone but he held it even further out of her reach. 'Give me the phone, Jack.'

'No.'

'Give me the phone or I'll scream again.'

'You scream again and I won't just kiss you this time,' he threatened darkly.

She let her arm drop by her side, her eyes widening at the look in his eyes. She couldn't make him out. He gave every appearance of being uncomfortable with her around, but as soon as she offered to leave he refused to let her go. What was going on?

'I see,' she said, even though she didn't.

She watched as he dragged a hand through his hair for the second time, giving him an out-of-character tousled look. She couldn't help noticing the dark bruise-like shadows beneath his eyes. He looked exhausted, as well he should considering he'd been on call two nights in a row, each of them stressful and technically demanding.

She suddenly felt ashamed of the fuss she was making. After all, he was only doing what any decent person would do, offering her a place to stay until things were sorted out at her flat. Most of her friends lived too far away from St Patrick's for it to be convenient, especially for her on-call shifts, and with Ben and her parents out of reach Jack was as close to family as she could get at short notice.

He handed her back the phone, his eyes avoiding hers. 'I'll organise to have your car fixed first thing in the morning. You should get some sleep—it's been a long night.'

She took the phone and stared at him for a moment or two, her fingers feeling where the warmth of his hand had been.

She was still trying to think of something to say when the telephone beside his bed rang.

He moved past her to answer it, turning his back to her. 'Colcannon.'

'Mr Colcannon,' Robert said. 'There have been a couple of admissions since you left. Sorry to call you so late but while they're not urgent, I just need some advice.'

'Of course, Robert,' Jack said. 'What have you got?''

'There's a Mrs Ryan who's had vomiting and pain in the right upper quadrant, going through to the back. She's tender in the upper abdomen, more on the right, but no mass, normal bowel sounds, slightly febrile. I think it sounds like acute cholecystitis. I've ordered an ultrasound.'

'Good, that's fine. Make sure you get bloods, including liver function tests, amylase and lipase, and start her on IV cephalosporin. What else have you got?'

'A male, mid-forties with suspected pancreatitis. He's a heavy drinker and presented with acute epigastric pain through to the back. His lipase is off the scale.'

'OK. Order a CT scan for the morning, put him in HDU for the rest of tonight, get him catheterised and make sure he's producing at least 30 mls an hour urine output. Repeat all his blood parameters and blood gases, and get a chest X-ray,' Jack advised.

'Thanks, got all that,' Robert said. 'The last one is an ischiorectal abscess in a seventy-year-old male. I've organised Theatre and the anaesthetic registrar is available, but if you want Dr Baxter to be called in…'

'No,' Jack said. 'The registrar can handle that and so can you. You've done enough draining of abscesses now to do that with one hand tied behind your back. Anything else?'

'There's a suspected appendix but we're going to sit on it till the morning. The patient isn't febrile and the symptoms are a bit vague. He's also been on a bit of a bender so it's hard to make a proper diagnosis.'

'Friday nights are like that,' Jack said, running his hand along the side of his jaw. 'Call me if there's anything urgent. I'll be in around eight for a quick round. Thank God I'm off for the rest of the weekend.'

'It's certainly been a big week,' Robert agreed.

'Tell me something I don't know,' Jack said, and rang off.

'Do you have to go back in?' Becky asked, hovering at the end of his bed.

He returned the phone to its cradle before answering. 'No, there's nothing urgent going on. I'll check things when I go in in the morning.'

'The night isn't over yet,' she said, smothering a yawn.

'It is as far as I'm concerned.' He sat on the edge of the bed and began to untie his shoe laces. 'Besides, Robert's turning out to be quite a good registrar. He'll let me know if anything needs my attention and he'll deal with the rest.'

Becky watched as he methodically placed his shoes side by side, his socks neatly folded, not scrunched up as she or Ben would have left them.

'You look tired,' she said after a small silence.

'Yeah, well, that's just how it looks on the outside.' He rubbed his hand over his eyes. 'You should feel it from where I'm feeling it.'

'Why do you work yourself so hard?'

He lifted his bloodshot gaze to her, his expression becoming distinctly exasperated. 'Why don't you go to bed like a good little house guest and leave me in peace?'

Becky sent him an arctic look, wishing she hadn't tried to be nice to him. 'You can be such a jerk sometimes.'

'Only sometimes?'

'All of the time.'

He got up and began unbuttoning his shirt.

'What are you doing?' She stared at him, her heart doing a little kick-start in her chest.

'I'm getting undressed, so if you want to see the rest, stick around,' he said, his hands going to his waistband to unbuckle his belt.

Becky wished she had the courage to call his bluff. It wasn't as if she hadn't seen the naked male form, she had—hundreds, if not thousands, of times—but Jack's was something else.

She turned on her heel and left his room, the sound of his laughter incensing her even further.

She locked herself in the bathroom and, rummaging through her hastily gathered toiletries, washed her face and cleaned her teeth. She changed into the T-shirt Jack had given her, looking at her reflection with a rueful grimace as she saw how the soft fabric outlined her figure rather too closely.

She sighed and turned on the taps to rinse out her lacy knickers and bra before hanging them over the shower cubicle to dry.

The spare room was decorated in the sort of everything-matching-nothing-out-of-place way she'd come to expect from Jack. With a mischievous little smile playing about her mouth, she went through the room and deliberately put things out of place, ruffling the perfect curtains, scrunching up the spare pillows and leaving her clothes and shoes in a scattered pile on the floor. She tilted the gilt-edged mirror above the antique dressing-table at a crazy angle, making sure her recently moisturised fingers left a decent-sized smudge.

She bounced on the bed a couple of times, knowing he

would probably hear it in the room next door but way past caring.

'Will you shut the hell up in there?' Jack's deep voice came through the wall. 'I'm trying to sleep!'

'Did you say something, Jack?' she cooed back, stretching languorously on the bed, one of her hands inadvertently knocking the electronic bedside clock to the floor. The radio came on at high volume, the shrieking of violin strings filling the silence with nerve-tightening sound.

'Oops!' She rolled off the bed, trying to find the 'off' switch, but all she managed to do was change stations and increase the volume. This time instead of violins the mind-numbing sound of techno music filled the room.

She was on the floor, still fiddling with the buttons, when Jack came bursting into the room, his face contorted with fury.

'What is it with you?' he growled, coming over to scoop the radio out of her hands and snapping it off.

Becky got up off the floor and straightened the T-shirt over her curves. 'I didn't mean to knock it off the table.'

He glared at her. 'And I don't suppose you meant to use the bed like a trampoline either?'

'I was checking the mattress,' she lied.

He gave her a disgusted look. 'And I bet you've tested a few of those in your time.'

Her mouth dropped open in outrage. 'You sexist pig! I bet you've dented a few as well!'

His jaw tightened. 'That's none of your business. Now, get in that bed and go to sleep before I—'

'Before you what, Jack?' she cut in before he could finish. 'Kiss me again? I know you want to. I can see it in your eyes.'

Jack held her taunting look for as long as he dared. He should never have kissed her. What the hell was Ben thinking? This was never going to work.

'You're imagining it,' he said, stepping away from her. 'I want nothing to do with you.'

He strode over to the door and slammed it shut behind him, the noise of wood and lock connecting making her flinch.

'Fine,' she muttered under her breath. 'I don't want anything to do with you either.'

She flopped back down on the bed and shut her eyes but, exhausted as she was, it took ages before she could relax enough to sleep.

CHAPTER SIX

JACK put down his cup of coffee as soon as Becky entered the kitchen the next morning. 'I was thinking about doing a quick ward round,' he said. 'Why don't you come with me for the ride?'

Becky gave him a quelling look as she picked up the coffee-pot. 'I can think of a hundred things I'd rather be doing than following you around the hospital while you check and double-check every patient's file, as if the only person who knows what they're doing in the whole hospital is you.'

'Yeah, well, I'm the one they sue if anything goes wrong,' he reminded her with undisguised bitterness.

'Don't you ever take a day off?' she asked, leaning back against the counter with her coffee cradled in her hands. 'You know, kick back and relax and forget all about being a surgeon for a while?'

Jack shifted his gaze from her scrutiny. 'I have time off.'

'When?'

'Tomorrow.'

'Well, bully for you, a day off,' she said with a curl of her lip. 'I wonder how you'll manage to fill in a whole twenty-four hours.'

Jack silently ground his teeth. This wasn't going to plan. He didn't want to leave Becky alone but neither did he want her trailing after him at the hospital, making her snide remarks on his working habits for all and sundry to hear. Ben had said to keep her with him at all times outside work but Jack knew she would be highly suspicious if he pressed her to join him on a ward round that he could just as easily get out of the way within minutes if he left now. If he waited for her to have a shower and do her hair, half the day would be over.

'I won't be at the hospital any longer than an hour,' he said. 'Don't answer the door.'

'I won't,' Becky promised. *Because I won't even be here,* she added mentally, smiling sweetly at him as he picked up his keys.

Once she was sure he was gone she went back upstairs to have a quick shower before throwing on her clothes. She gathered her few things together in a carry bag, turned off her mobile and made her way outside to wait for the taxi she'd called earlier. She asked the driver to drop her off in the city and went into the first reasonably priced hotel she came to.

'How many nights would you like to check in for?' the young woman at Reception asked.

'Um…the weekend to start with.' Becky did a quick mental tally of her credit-card account and crossed her fingers behind her back.

'Will anyone else be joining you?' The young woman handed her the registration forms to fill in.

Becky hated this part. It never failed to make her feel spinsterish and left on the shelf.

She gave the woman a little smile. 'I'm not sure, but who knows? A girl can get lucky in a big city.'

The receptionist smiled politely but it didn't reach her carefully made-up eyes. 'I hope you enjoy your stay with us. If there is anything we can do to make your time more comfortable, please let us know.'

'Thank you.'

'I'll get the porter to take your luggage to your room.'

'I don't have any luggage just yet,' Becky said. 'I'm going shopping right now to get some.'

The receptionist's eyebrows went up just a fraction but to her credit she didn't respond. Becky pocketed the swipe card key and left.

The shops were clogged with Christmas shoppers, which made the task of replenishing her wardrobe all the more time-consuming. The queues were interminably long, the staff considerably stressed and the spirit of Christmas nowhere to be found in the sticky heat that infiltrated the stores in spite of air-conditioning.

By midmorning Becky only had a couple of changes of clothes, some overpriced-but-to-die-for underwear and a pink and white bikini she couldn't resist buying on impulse. She stopped to have a manicure because of the free offer of hand lotion and lip gloss, and as she walked past the cosmetics counter she agreed to have a mini-facial in order to get the special deal on moisturiser.

At two p.m. she had a double caramel lattè and a slice of raspberry cheesecake in a café and turned on her phone to check for messages. The first three were from Jack but the other number she didn't recognise. She pressed the replay buttons and listened to each message in turn.

'Rebec..Becky, where the hell are you?' Jack's tone was clipped with anger. 'Call me immediately.'

She deleted it and pressed for the next message to play.

'So help me, God, if you don't tell me where you are, Rebecca Baxter, I won't be answerable for the consequences. *Call me now!*'

She deleted it with considerable relish and pressed the next one.

'Right.' Jack's tone was now livid. 'I don't know what game you are playing at, young lady, but when I find you I'm going to make you regret it big time. If you don't call me in the next hour I'm going to hire a bloody private investigator to find you. *Do you hear me?*'

'Loud and clear.' Becky grinned as she pressed the 'delete' button.

The fourth message was from the police officer who had attended her call about the burglary.

'Hello, Dr Baxter, this is Constable Matthew Daniels. I was wondering if you could give me a call at your convenience. There are a few questions I'd like to ask you about the robbery investigation. My mobile number is as follows...'

Becky saved the message and pressed 'recall'. It answered on the second ring.

'Constable Daniels.'

'Hi, this is Becky Baxter here. You called me earlier?'

'Hello, Dr Baxter,' he greeted her warmly. 'Thanks for getting back to me.'

'No trouble,' she said pleasantly. 'What can I do for you? You said you had some questions for me about the investigation.'

'Yes. I was wondering if I could meet you later this evening to go over them with you, what, say, about seven? Would that be convenient?'

'Sure,' she said. 'I've got nothing planned.'

'I'll pick you up,' he offered politely. 'What's your current address?'

'I'm staying at a hotel in the city,' she told him. 'The Principal On The Park. Room 1205.'

'That was good thinking on your part,' he said. 'Twenty-four hour security.'

'Yes…' She gnawed her bottom lip for a moment. 'Have you got any leads on the case, Constable Daniels?'

'Please, call me Matt.'

'Only if you'll call me Becky,' she said. 'Everyone else does.' *Well, almost everyone.*

'Becky, then,' he said. 'As to the case, I'd rather discuss that with you in person.' There was a small pause before he added, 'Off the record, so to speak.'

'Oh.'

'Will I meet you in the bar or in your room?' he asked.

'The bar will be fine.' She had a sudden thought and added, 'Unless you'll be in uniform? Maybe you'd prefer…'

'I won't be in uniform and the bar is fine,' he said. 'See you at seven.'

Becky had her finger poised over the turn-off switch when her phone began to ring. Jack's number flashed on the screen and her finger hovered for a moment in indecision. Several people looked up from their tables to glare at her and she turned her back and answered it, knowing she was probably going to regret it.

'Could you hold for a moment?' she said, hastily clutching the phone to her breast to smother Jack's cursing protest.

She scooped up her things and quickly left the café, leaving some money for her snack on the counter on the way past.

She stood to one side of the busy pavement and held the phone up to her ear. 'Hello, Becky here.'

'Where the freaking hell are you?'

'Shopping.'

'Shopping?'

'Yes, you know that activity that women love and men hate? The one where lots of money changes hands in exchange for the latest fashion and accessories?'

'If you had *any* idea of how furious I am with you right now you wouldn't be able to stand upright for the quaking of your legs,' he ground out.

'Ooh! I am *so* scared,' she goaded him.

His one sharp swear word made her eyebrows lift momentarily and a funny sensation flickered between her thighs, making her legs feel a little unstable all of a sudden.

'I've been out of my mind for the past six hours!' he went on heatedly. 'You didn't even leave a note. I had no idea what had happened to you.'

'Why should you care?' she said. 'It's not as if you really want me staying at your house. You've made it more than clear I'm just a total nuisance.'

'You're not a nuisance, you're a bloody nightmare,' he muttered darkly.

'Well, lucky for you I have somewhere else to stay now, so you can keep your pathetic attempt at hospitality and shove it down your—'

'Where are you staying?' he barked at her.

'Wouldn't you like to know?' she tossed back.

'Tell me where you're staying,' he demanded, his voice rising.

'Stop shouting at me.'

'I am *not* shouting at you!' he shouted. 'Tell me where you are, for pity's sake!'

'I'm staying at a hotel.'

'Where?'

'I'm not telling you.'

Jack gritted his teeth in frustration as he tried to calm down. No one, but no one, made him as angry as Becky. His blood virtually pumped with it, making him as tense as a tightly stretched wire. He could barely think straight when she was around, and when she wasn't…well, he couldn't think at all.

He'd promised Ben that he'd look after her but he was doing a poor job of it so far. She'd slipped out of his sight, totally unaware of the extreme danger she was in. He'd thought of warning her about it on one of his messages but decided Ben was probably right. It would only frighten her and she'd already had two terrifying episodes to deal with as it was.

'Look…' He tried another tack. 'Can we have dinner tonight?'

'*Dinner?*' Her tone was incredulous.

'Yeah,' he said dryly. 'That activity that couples do from time to time, where large amounts of money are exchanged for a meal you could have cooked for a fraction of the price at home.'

'We are not a couple,' she said. 'And, besides, I'm already busy tonight.'

He frowned. 'Doing what?'

'I'm going on a date.'

'With whom?'

'A man.'

'What man?'

'No one you know.'

Jack's stomach gave a disturbing clench.

'Is it someone from the hospital?' he asked after a short silence.

'No.'

'How well do you know this guy?'

'What is this?' she asked disdainfully. 'Twenty Questions?'

'Who the hell are you going out with?' His voice rose once more.

'He's a cop.'

'*A cop?*' he choked.

Becky rolled her eyes and stepped out of the way of a determined shopper. 'What's the matter with you, Jack? He's one of the good guys.'

'How do you know?'

'Oh, for God's sake!' she said in exasperation. 'I already have a father and a big brother so quit it with the protective male relative routine, OK?'

'I can't help feeling responsible for you.'

'I can't imagine why.'

'Well, for a start, you're a walking, breathing disaster,' he said. 'Apart from when you're at work, where you are surprisingly highly competent and professional, but for some reason once you leave the premises you turn into an airhead.'

'Has anyone told you lately how much of a pain in the butt you are?' she snapped.

'I think you were the last person to do so.'

'I'm hanging up,' she said.

'If you hang up, I swear to God I'll—'

Becky hung up and switched off her phone, stuffing it in her bag with a determined shove of her hand.

She strode off into the nearest boutique and bought an outfit that cost a fortune, and didn't even blink an eye when the transaction was processed. With the rest of her purchases in each hand she went back to her hotel, ordered a hot snack from room service and ate it while she lay in the spa, using a host of free samples she'd been given at the cosmetics counter.

'I hate him,' she addressed the fragrant bubbles in front of her. 'He's a complete and utter Neanderthal.' She popped another French fry into her mouth and chewed it savagely. 'I hate him for being such a control freak. I hate him for being so…' She choked back a tiny sob. 'I hate him for being so…so damn un-hatable.'

Jack had a gut feeling she was in the city. Although there was a huge shopping complex at Bondi Junction, he thought he'd heard the distinctive whirr of the city's monorail among the sounds of carol singers and the general hustle and bustle of the busy crowds as he'd been talking to her on the phone.

The only problem was, the city was full of hotels. It would take him hours to call each one and even then privacy protocol was such that they might not tell him her room number.

He decided to think like a cop. Ben would be good at this, he thought as he walked the length of the city. He would narrow it down to the area he thought she would be most interested in shopping in. Not only that, city hotels were not cheap and she was a staff anaesthetist after all. She wouldn't be throwing money away unnecessarily, particularly as she had just been robbed and needed to replace what she could, and it could take weeks before the insurance claim was processed.

He decided she would most probably choose a hotel a couple of blocks from town, maybe somewhere up the far end of Hyde Park. The lush green of the trees along the Walk of Remembrance would appeal to her sense of sentimentality, not to mention the Pool of Reflection near the War Memorial. He decided she probably wouldn't go for harbour views as it would push the price up too much, although one could never be too sure with Becky. As far as impulsiveness went, she more or less took the cake.

At the first three hotels he drew a blank. But he got lucky on the fourth.

Becky gave her freshly dried hair a last quick pat and reapplied her new strawberry lip gloss. She sprayed herself liberally with her new perfume, which had been on sale with a bonus gift of a make-up travel kit. She ran her hands down her slinky hot-pink dress with the diamanteé shoestring straps, her heels giving her some of the height Ben had selfishly stolen from her at the Baxter genetic door.

Matt Daniels rose from his seat in the piano bar as she approached, a smile spreading over his face as she slipped her hand into his.

'You look completely different without your uniform,' she said.

His warm brown eyes swept over her in undisguised male appraisal. 'You're looking pretty good yourself.'

'Thank you.'

He held out a chair for her in a quiet corner. 'What would you like to drink?'

Becky really had no head for alcohol and as a general rule avoided it, but somehow tonight she felt a little bit more daring than usual. Although she had absolutely no idea what it contained, she asked for the first cocktail she saw on the list above the bar.

'I'll have an Abracadabra,' she said.

The drinks waiter took Matt's order for a light beer and discreetly moved away.

'So.' Matt leaned forward, his arms resting on his knees. 'How are you holding up?'

Becky gave him a wavering smile. 'I'm doing OK.'

'No panic attacks or sleepless nights?'

Her expression instantly became rueful. 'My bank manager would probably prefer it if I did, but, no, my number-one coping mechanism is to shop. It works every time.'

He smiled, his eyes crinkling in the corners. 'I have a sister just like you.'

'You do?'

He nodded and leaned back as their drinks arrived. He paid for them and waited until the waiter had left before continuing, 'My sister Penny has a black belt in shopping.'

Becky grinned and reached for her drink. 'Yeah? Well, I'm working my way up to a PhD in purchasing. After today I figure I'm almost there.'

He gave her an amused smile and took a sip of his beer. 'Do you have any family?'

'My parents are overseas just now,' she said, twirling her straw. 'They're celebrating being married for thirty-five years with a six-week cruise and a white Christmas in Europe.'

'Wow, that's some innings for a marriage these days.'

'Yes.' She gave him another little smile. 'I have a brother, too.'

'What does he do?'

'You're not going to believe this, but he's a cop.'

'No kidding?' He took another swig of his beer. 'What branch?'

Becky always found it hard to exactly describe what her brother did. He was guarded about the details, as if by telling his family what he did was going to somehow compromise him.

'He moves around a bit,' she hedged. 'He's been in traffic, then accident investigation and now I think he's doing a stint in the drug squad.'

'Tough call,' Matt said.

'That sounds like the voice of experience,' she observed.

He gave her a twisted smile. 'I've moved around a bit, too. You see it all eventually.'

She gave her straw another twirl. 'It's not an easy job, being a cop.'

'No, but sometimes you get results and it makes it all worthwhile,' he said.

She set her drink to one side, not sure she really liked the taste of it in spite of its colourful umbrella and little kebab stick of tropical fruit.

'So.' She met his eyes once more. 'What did you want to ask me?'

He leaned forward in his chair. 'There's something about the robbery and the intruder that doesn't quite add up.'

'What do you mean?'

He glanced around the bar as if he expected someone to be listening in. Becky couldn't help noticing the likeness to Ben. Once a cop always a cop, she thought as she leaned in closer to hear.

'I could be wrong, but I don't think the robber and the intruder are the same guy,' Matt said in a low voice.

Becky reached for her drink, for something to do with her suddenly twitchy hands. 'You don't?'

He shook his head.

'Who do you think it is?'

He pursed his lips for a moment. 'I'm not sure.'

She swallowed. 'You mean *two* people are after me?'

'I wouldn't go as far as saying someone's after you. The two incidents could very well prove to be totally unconnected.'

'If that's supposed to give me peace of mind, let me tell you it hasn't quite done the job.'

'No, I imagine not,' he said. 'Being burgled is a violating experience but having an intruder looking at you in the middle of the night is something else again.'

'Tell me about it.' She suppressed a shudder and took another sip of her drink, doing her best not to screw up her face at the taste.

'I had an unmarked car drive by your place a few times last night but so far nothing has come up that's in any way suspicious.'

'Thank you,' she said. 'I really appreciate it.'

'There's been a spate of burglaries in your area lately,' he said. 'It's not always the case, of course, but as a general rule we often find the same gang is responsible for each of the break-ins. They do an area and then move on to somewhere else.'

'You think my break-in was the work of a locally operating gang?'

He gave her a lengthy look. 'On first appearances it would appear to be a straightforward forced entry and quick grab for goods, but...'

'But?' she prompted.

'That scrawl in lipstick on the mirror.' He gave her an unblinking look. 'Is there anyone in your life you suspect of ill feeling towards you? I know you've been asked that before but sometimes it takes a while for it to sink in.'

A vision of Jack flitted into her mind but she just as quickly dismissed it.

'No.'

'Are you sure?'

She met his concerned gaze and was again reminded of her brother. It seemed as if cops were all the same, no matter what their rank.

'Look, I'm the first to admit I don't have the best track record where relationships are concerned,' she confessed with a little grimace. 'I've been engaged three times, but I'm absolutely sure none of my ex-fiancés would hold anything against me. Believe me, revenge would be the last thing on their minds. All they wanted was their freedom. I haven't heard from any of them for years.'

'Have you had anything else happen to you lately that could be considered a little suspicious?' he asked.

She chewed her lip for a moment then told him, 'I've had three flat tyres over the last week, and my tyres were slashed yesterday in the hospital car park.'

'Did you report all that?'

She shook her head. 'I was going to, but...'

'But?'

'I didn't want to face it, I guess,' she said. 'I'm not used to thinking of myself as a victim of crime.'

'You're not alone in that,' he said. 'No one wants to face such a prospect, but it happens all the same.'

'Yes, I know.'

'Does anyone else know you're staying here?'

She lifted her gaze to his. 'No. I haven't told anyone but you.'

'Good.' He looked relieved. 'Let's keep it that way for a while. I'm working on a few leads and it would suit me if no one knows where you are spending the night. If anyone needs to contact you, let them do it via your mobile.'

'But I gave my name at Reception. If anyone asks...'

'Put a block on it,' he said. 'Tell Reception you don't want your details handed out. I can do it for you on my way out if you like. You'd be amazed at what a flash of a badge can achieve.'

'Oh, would you?' She gave him a grateful look. 'I'm pathetic at all this cloak-and-dagger stuff.'

He gave her a reassuring smile. 'Let's hope none of this turns out to be in that category. For all we know, this is probably a simple case of mistaken identity or at the very least a straightforward break and entry.'

'I certainly hope you're right,' she said, taking another sip of her loathsome drink. 'I don't like to think of myself as somebody's target practice.'

'Random acts of violence are thankfully very rare. Statistics show that most victims of violent crime have known the perpetrator in some way.'

'So what you're saying is I'm somehow connected to these people?'

He gave her a brief look as he set his empty glass down. 'Suffice it to say I'm not ruling it out.'

'Great,' she said wryly. 'And I just sent off all my Christmas cards, too.'

'Want me to run a check on all the names?' he offered.

'No,' she said. 'But I'm going to have a serious rethink about my Christmas shopping.'

He stood up to leave, offering her his hand with a friendly smile. 'You really should meet my sister,' he said.

She returned his smile with one of her own. 'And you definitely should meet my brother.'

'You never know,' he said with an inscrutable little smile. 'Maybe I already have.'

Becky opened her mouth to respond but he'd already turned and slipped away.

CHAPTER SEVEN

BECKY swiped her card key and opened the door of her suite only to come up short when a tall dark figure rose from the sofa as the door closed behind her.

'How did you get in here?' she gasped as Jack stepped towards her.

He held up a swipe card in two long, tanned fingers, his green eyes locking on to hers.

'I told the person at Reception I was your husband.'

'*What?*'

He smiled a self-satisfied smile. 'I don't think they believed me at first—they weren't too keen to let me in—but I managed to convince them in the end.'

'How?' She eyeballed him suspiciously, wondering what he had done that could have gone beyond the authority of Matt Daniels's police badge.

He took out his wallet and waved a hundred-dollar note in front of her nose.

'You bastard!' She slapped at his hand in anger. 'How dare you invade my privacy? You had no right!'

He captured her hand and tugged her towards him, his eyes glittering dangerously. 'I told you I'd track you down and now I have.'

'Let me go!' She pulled against his hold but it was so firm she could feel the steady beat of his heart underneath her flattened palm, making her pulse kick up to a breakneck pace.

'Why did you disappear like that?' he asked.

'It's none of your business.' She gave him a glare. 'I don't have to answer to you.'

'I beg to differ, young lady,' he said, his fingers tightening a fraction around hers. 'Don't forget you still owe me for the replacement of my bumper, not to mention the renewal of your four tyres, which I paid for this morning, as well as the towing fee to the repair shop.'

She felt her stomach drop as she thought of her credit-card limit, and wished she hadn't been quite so reckless with her purchases that day. The dress she was wearing was worth at least two of his stupid bumpers, and just one of her shoes would have paid for a tyre at the very least.

'I'll pay you back every cent,' she said. 'Now, get out of here before I call the police.'

'Ah, yes.' His top lip curled back in scorn. 'That reminds me. How was your little date with the man in blue?'

She clamped her lips together, refusing to answer him.

'I must say he didn't stay long,' he mused. 'One drink and he was gone.'

Her mouth dropped open and her eyes widened in affront. *'You were watching?'*

The self-satisfied smile returned. 'I was expecting you to bring lover boy up here. What's wrong, Becky, losing your touch?'

Her eyes flashed at him in fury. 'Do you know how much I loathe and detest you?'

'I have a fair idea, but quite frankly it doesn't bother me all that much.'

'I don't think there is a single thing you could do either now or any time in the future to make me hate you more than I do right at this moment,' she said through tight lips.

'Good,' he said, suddenly pulling her even closer. 'Then you won't hate me any more for doing this.'

His eyes held hers for two or three heartbeats, which should have been enough warning but somehow wasn't. Her startled gasp disappeared into the warm cave of his mouth as it connected with hers with bruising force, her limbs going to water at the first determined thrust of his tongue as it arrogantly hunted down hers.

Becky felt the draining away of her resistance as if someone had suddenly pulled a plug within her, leaving her totally at the mercy of her urgent, desperate need for the sensory overload his hard, angry kiss was stoking within her. She could feel it flying with scorching heat along the pathways of her veins, the deep heady throb of it coming to a pulsating point of aching pressure between her legs where one of his hard muscled thighs had moved in to separate them.

His kiss became all the more determined, leaving no corner of her trembling mouth unexplored. She felt herself being swept away on a great wave of feeling, the pressure of his aroused body on the soft yielding of hers too much for her to withstand. She felt the sag of her legs even as he half lifted, half pushed her towards the bed behind her, the collapse of their combined weight on the mattress sending her breath out of her lungs in a startled gasp of pure pleasure as his hard frame moulded itself to hers, his angles fitting neatly into her curves while his tongue duelled hungrily with hers.

Jack wasn't sure exactly who was kissing whom. He had started this in anger but he wasn't feeling angry any more. What he was feeling now was a need so strong it was threatening to take over every moral boundary he'd constructed in the past to keep him from putting his hands on his best friend's little sister. She was in his arms and responding to him in a way he had not realised he'd wanted until he'd felt it again, just the way he'd felt it twelve years ago, just the way he'd felt it when he'd kissed her to shut her up—had it really only been yesterday? He didn't know or care. All he knew was that his body wanted her with a fierce, out-of-control desire, and nothing could stop him from consummating it right here and now.

With his mouth still locked to hers, he shifted the tiny sparkling straps of her dress to one side, his hand covering her revealed breast, his lower stomach tilting in sharp pleasure at the feel of her soft perfection, the tight bud of her nipple driving into the bed of his palm.

He felt her squirming beneath him, her body's instinctive movements thrilling him in a way no one had ever done before. He'd always kept himself slightly aloof from the emotional aspect of physical union, seeing it as something that could only complicate and blur the edges of reason in a casual relationship. But with Becky in his arms it felt different, as if she had somehow crawled under his skin and made it feel alive in a way it had never felt before. He felt it when her hands skimmed the muscles of his back, he felt it when her fingers dug into his buttocks to bring him even closer, he felt it when she undid his waistband and freed him into her hands.

'Oh, no,' he groaned, placing his hand on hers, the pulse of his erection still beneath her fingers.

She blinked up at him with wide uncertain eyes and he gritted his teeth and rolled off her, keeping her hand on him as consolation to his untimely overactive conscience.

'This is all wrong.' He put his free hand up to his eyes to cover them.

She splayed her fingers, which produced another deep agonised groan from his throat, but his hand kept hers in place regardless.

He uncovered his eyes and turned his head to look at her. 'Do you realise how close I am to following through on this?'

Becky moistened her lips with her tongue, not sure what to say. A few moments ago she'd been furious with him, but now…

'Becky…' He hitched himself up on one elbow and turned his upper body toward her, leaving her caressing hand where it was.

Becky moved her fingers once more, stroking the hard pulsing length of him, revelling in the dark glitter of desire her actions produced in his eyes as they held hers.

She traced her fingertip over his moistened tip, watching in awe as his features contorted with pleasure at her touch. He was like silk-encased steel under her caress, his body totally under her command, her feminine power apparent to her in a way it had never been before.

She knew then, as if someone sitting on her shoulder had just whispered it in her ear. She had been waiting for this moment ever since she'd been seventeen when his hard mouth had crushed down onto hers in a kiss of hot fire and frustration.

No wonder her three attempts at being engaged had failed! How could she fall in love with another man when all this time she'd been in love with Jack Colcannon?

In love with Jack...

She drew in a tiny breath as her fingers curled around him, the realisation of her feelings making her glow inside with liquid warmth.

She loved him.

'We have to stop this right now.' Although Jack's tone was determined, he did nothing to move out of her reach. 'It's total madness.'

She slowly lifted her luminous eyes to his. 'Why do we have to stop?'

His dark brows drew together momentarily. 'What are you saying, Becky—that you want to continue?'

She let her fingers do the talking and he sucked in a prickly breath, his body as tense as a tightly bound spring.

'Wouldn't it be nice if just for once we stopped arguing and tried another way of communicating?' she said softly, her caresses becoming bolder.

He ran his tongue over his dry mouth, staring at the fullness of hers as his blood charged through his body at turbo speed. He could almost feel her mouth on him, her little cat-like tongue...

With a strength he'd not known he'd possessed he wrenched himself out of her hold and got off the bed, tucking himself back into his trousers, his breathing still choppy as he put some distance between them. He scored a pathway through his hair with one hand and began to pace the room agitatedly, rubbing his jaw, cracking his knuckles, all the time avoiding her eyes.

Becky felt his rejection as if he'd slapped her with it. Shame ran like a hot red tide through her, completing its journey by settling in twin circles on her cheeks. She could see the undisguised distaste for her etched on his features. Even the line of his mouth was grim.

She got off the bed and straightened her straps with as much dignity as she could gather. It was spread pretty thinly.

'OK, so it looks like we continue with the arguing,' she said dryly. 'Where were we? Was it my turn to throw a verbal punch or yours?'

He stopped pacing to look at her. 'If it's any salve to your pride I *was* going to sleep with you. I've never been that close to losing control before.'

'Well, congratulations for withstanding the temptation,' she bit out. 'You really know how to make a girl feel irresistible.'

He frowned as she stalked across the room to pick up her shoes, her movements stiff with injured pride.

'Look, I don't want you to think I'm not attracted to you.'

She turned back to face him, shoes in hand. 'What are you scared of, Jack, that I might ask you for an engagement ring?'

'No, of course not, it's just…difficult.'

'Look, why don't you just leave right now before you make it any worse? I get the message. You don't have to wrap it up to make it more palatable.'

'Becky.' He turned her around to face him, his hands on her upper arms, his eyes holding hers. 'Believe me, you'll thank me for this in the morning. You've been under a lot of strain and you're not thinking clearly right now.' He gave her arms a little squeeze. 'You hate me, remember? What sort of guy would I be if I slept with you, knowing that?'

It was on the tip of her tongue to vehemently deny it but she stopped herself at the last moment. It was clear he felt nothing for her, so what would be the point of revealing her feelings for him? For years she'd actively demonstrated her dislike of him, had practically made it her life's work to annoy him. Telling him she loved him now would be nothing less than emotional suicide.

'You're right.' She gave him a self-deprecating smile. 'I'm not myself right now. God, what was I thinking? You are *so* not my type.' She eased herself out of his hold. 'Under normal circumstances you are the very last man on earth I would ever think of sleeping with.' She forced a laugh and moved her shoulders in what she hoped looked like a physical cringe. 'I wonder what was in that cocktail I had downstairs. Ben's always saying how alcohol impairs one's judgement. It must have been totally loaded.'

Not as loaded as the gun he'd just shot himself in the foot with, Jack thought wryly as he watched the relief wash over her features.

'It can get expensive, staying in hotels for extended periods,' he said, finally finding his voice. 'Wouldn't it be better to stay at my place until your place is cleaned up?'

She gave him one of her you've-got-to-be-joking looks. 'I'm only staying until I get another flat. I don't think I want to live in that one any more.'

Jack knew it wasn't exactly ideal, but at least the hotel had twenty-four-hour security, and another hundred bucks should keep the front desk silent over her presence in room 1205. And maybe another hundred would get them to call him if she happened to mention where she intended to go on her day off tomorrow.

'Your car won't be ready until late next week,' he informed her, handing her a card with the workshop's address and phone number. 'The mechanic wanted to check a few things first.' He didn't tell her he'd had to insist on the mechanic keeping it longer than necessary, but until he ruled out foul play he wasn't going to take any chances.

'Thank you,' she said, lowering her gaze a fraction. 'I don't know how I'll ever repay you.'

'Well…see you later, then,' he said, his hand hesitating on the doorknob.

She plastered a bright smile on her face. 'See you, Jack. And thank you for not…taking advantage of me. I really appreciate it. You don't know how much.'

He left without another word, somehow feeling she'd got the last one in anyway.

*　　*　　*

Becky tucked her sunscreen back in her tote bag and surveyed the sparkling ocean in front of her, her skin still tingling with the feel of the salt water after her short dip to christen her new bikini.

Bondi Beach had more than its usual Sunday-in-December crowd, the intense heat wave bringing in even more from the outlying suburbs.

She lay back on her towel and turned her head, squinting against the sunlight. She'd hardly slept last night after Jack had left, and the sun was so warm and the sound of happy bathers so soothing she closed her eyes and let the delicious warmth dry up the sea's moisture on her skin and seep right into her bones...

'Help! Help, somebody, please!'

She jerked upright at the sound of the desperate plea coming from a few feet away.

A little girl of about ten or so was shaking in terror as she stood over the convulsing form of her mother in the sand.

Becky sprang to her feet and ran to the terrified girl. 'What happened?'

'My mummy. She's a diabetic. I think she's got her insulin dose wrong. She's fitted once before,' wailed the distraught child.

Becky turned the woman onto her side into the coma position and pulled her jaw forward to help clear her airway.

'Can someone call triple 0?' she called into the gathering crowd.

The woman began convulsive fitting again, becoming cyanosed, with frothing saliva and a little blood from a lacerated lip, while her daughter sobbed in distress in the background, answering Becky's quick questions through tears.

'Can anyone here get a first-aid kit from the lifeguard station?' Becky shouted into the sea of fascinated faces.

In front of her the crowd started to separate as a dark, tall figure in black bathers pushed through with a plastic medical kit and an air of confidence she had seen many times before.

'Jack!' She stared up at him with a combination of relief and surprise. 'Are you tailing me or something?'

'Don't be ridiculous. I always swim here. What's wrong with this patient?'

'She's hypoglycaemic—too much insulin, no food and a little dehydrated.'

'There's IV gear and glucose in here,' Jack said as he opened the lifeguard's medical bag.

'Hold her arm still while I get in a cannula,' Becky instructed one of the lifeguards, who had accompanied Jack.

She inserted the only size cannula present in the kit, drew up 20 ml of ten per cent glucose into a syringe and injected it into the cannula. She repeated the manoeuvre three times until about 80 ml had been given. Suddenly the convulsions ceased, and after a few minutes, much to the relief of the onlooking crowd, and the sobbing thankfulness of the young daughter, the woman regained consciousness.

Within a few minutes an ambulance had picked up the patient and her daughter for transport to the local district hospital, the crowd dispersing back to their beach towels and umbrellas and the lifeguards returning to their lookout point.

Becky waited until the ambulance had gone before turning to Jack. 'I suppose you're going to tell me it's just a coincidence you were here this morning?'

'I told you, I often come down for a swim on Sundays,' he informed her evenly. It was more or less the truth, but the tip-off from the bell boy at the hotel had been a godsend, and well worth the expense. He gave the crowded beach a sweeping glance before coming back to her suspicious gaze. 'Along with the rest of the population.'

'I don't need a bodyguard,' she said, spinning on her heel to make her way back to her towel and bag. 'And even if I did, I don't think you're the person for the job.'

She shook off the sand on her towel and carefully straightened it before lying back down, closing her eyes, effectively shutting him out.

'Have you got sunscreen on?' he asked.

She opened one eye at him. 'I have all the protection I need.'

'If you ask me, you're starting to look a little pink.'

'I didn't ask you.' She flopped over onto her stomach and buried her head under her hat.

'Just here...' One of his fingers traced a light-fingered pathway over the top of her left shoulder.

'Stop it.' She wriggled under his touch. 'That tickles.'

'You shouldn't overdo it, you know,' he cautioned. 'A few minutes too long and you'll burn to a crisp.'

She angled her head to meet his eyes. 'Why don't you go and pick on somebody with fair skin?'

He smiled, his white teeth standing out against his deep olive tan. 'You might tan easily enough but it's not wise to try and do it in one day. I think you should reapply some sunscreen. I've taken off enough melanomas to know.'

'I think you should leave before I stuff the aforementioned sunscreen right down your throat.'

He threw back his head and laughed, bringing her head up off the towel to gape at him. When was the last time she'd heard him laugh? Truly laugh? Her stomach quivered at the sound of it, her legs feeling squishy all of a sudden.

'Here.' He reached for her bag. 'Get it out and I'll do your back, then I promise I'll go away and leave you alone.'

She rummaged in her tote bag and grudgingly handed the sunscreen to him, knowing she wasn't going to get rid of him any other way.

Jack looked down at the bottle, turning it over in his hands to see what exposure time the brand recommended.

His fingers stilled on the bottle as he read the handwritten label which had been placed over the manufacturer's directions.

YOU ARE GOING TO NEED MUCH MORE PROTECTION THAN THIS BITCH FACE

Becky swivelled her head to look at him, wondering why it was taking him so long to get the lid off.

'What's the matter? Isn't 30 plus enough to satisfy your perfectionist standards?'

He covered the makeshift label with his hand and squeezed out some of the lotion into his palm.

'No tan is a safe tan,' he said, absently smoothing some of it over the curve of her spine while his eyes quickly but thoroughly scanned the crowded beach.

Becky could sense his aversion to touching her and after a few moments slapped his hand away. Rolling over to sit up, she snatched her sunscreen out of his hand, glaring at him in affront.

'I wouldn't want to put you to any bother. I can see you've got much better things to do than...' Her words trailed away as she saw how his eyes dropped to the bottle in her hands as if it were a bomb waiting to go off.

She looked down at the label and froze.

CHAPTER EIGHT

SHE gulped back a swallow and looked up at Jack, the bottle falling from her fingers to the sand. 'He's here?'

Jack's eyes quickly scanned the beach on both sides, his stomach tightening at the thought of Becky's stalker hiding among the massive crowd.

'I'm not sure,' he answered, and turned to look at her, his eyes narrowed against the sunlight. 'When was the last time you put sunscreen on?'

She chewed her lip for a moment. 'I put it on before I went for a swim. I didn't reapply it after I came out. I was going to but then the little girl cried out for help.' She stared at her tote bag. 'I left my things here. Anyone could have come up and taken them, tampered with them...' She moistened her dry mouth as she reached for her bag to find her phone. 'We'd better call the police.'

'No!' His hand came down over hers.

She looked up at him in confusion. 'No?'

He removed his hand from hers, his eyes determined as they held hers. 'I don't think there's anything they can do. It's not as if they could identify anyone's footprints in this crowd.'

She looked at the stirred-up sand around her. Just to add credibility to Jack's statement, a teenage boy suddenly lunged right in front of them for the Frisbee his friend had thrown, stirring up a cloud of sand.

She dusted it off her legs and ankles and turned to look at Jack once more. 'I'm sort of over the whole beach thing right now.'

'Come on.' He hauled her to her feet with a strong hand. 'How did you get here? By bus?'

90

She nodded, looking away in embarrassment. 'I couldn't afford a taxi.'

'No problem,' he said taking her hand. 'We can walk to my house and I'll drive you back to the hotel.'

She curled her fingers into his and followed him without a word, somehow feeling relieved that he was by her side and in control.

They were silent in the hotel lift as it took them up to her room. Becky stared at the sand between her toes and wondered what had happened to her life. A couple of weeks ago she had been planning for a quieter than normal Christmas, now she was planning on staying alive.

'I'm scared,' she announced into the silence, still staring down at her scarlet-painted toenails.

Jack put an arm around her shoulders and drew her close. 'I know.'

Becky nestled into his solid frame, her head turning into his chest as she breathed in the familiar scent of him.

'You'll get through this, Becky,' he said into her hair. 'I know you will.'

'I wish I had your confidence,' she said, fingering one of the buttons on his casual surf shirt.

His hand went to the back of her head, his fingers burying into the silk of her hair. She felt his indrawn breath against her breasts as he pressed her even closer, close enough to feel the growing pulse of his arousal where it pressed against her stomach.

'I think we should empty out your flat this afternoon and move you temporarily into my place,' he said, easing himself away from her.

'Do you think that's such a good idea?' She looked up at him. 'We'll argue all the time. You know what we're like.'

'Then we'll have to call a truce,' he said.

'How long do you think that will last?' She gave him a sceptical glance as she stepped out of the lift on her floor.

'Look, once all this blows over you can get another apartment somewhere and things will go back to normal. I'm not asking you to live with me forever. Heaven knows, if I did, one or both of us would go stark raving mad.'

She swiped her card in the lock with unnecessary force and shoved open the door, tossing her wet sandy towel to one side and her tote bag to the other.

'OK, so maybe I could have put that a little better,' he conceded as she stalked off to the bathroom. 'What I meant was—'

'You know something, Jack?' She swung round and stood with her hands on her hips, glaring at him. 'Whatever charm school you enrolled in ripped you off. You don't know how to open your mouth without an insult falling out.'

'How have I insulted you?' He gave a look of exasperation. 'I'm doing my level best to help you.'

'Yeah, well, I'd really like to know what your motive is,' she said, scooping up her cosmetics and stuffing them into a carrier bag. She pushed past him at the bathroom door and haphazardly threw the rest of her things together.

'What do you mean by that?' he asked, turning around to follow her jerky, agitated movements as she packed.

She sent him an icy stare over one shoulder.

'You're only offering to help me as long as it doesn't inconvenience you. You don't want anyone at the hospital to know about us living together, albeit temporarily, and now you don't want me to call the police even though I've quite obviously been threatened again. What's going on?'

'Nothing. Nothing's going on.'

Her brown gaze glinted at him with growing suspicion. 'You know something about this, don't you?'

'Don't be ridiculous, Becky. You're imagining things,' he said, looking away. 'I'm just doing what your family would expect me to do in their absence.'

She narrowed her eyes. 'Have you talked to any of them about this?'

Jack hated lying to her but knew he had no choice. It wasn't just her life that was in danger, but Ben's as well.

'Talked to them? I don't even know where any of your family is right now.'

'You'd better not be lying to me, Jack, because if you are I'm going to be very, very angry.'

'I can deal with your anger,' he said, turning back to look at her. 'I'm more or less used to it. Now, let's get moving. I have to go in to the hospital this evening to check on a patient in HDU.'

He heard her mutter something under her breath about him being a workaholic but he chose this time to ignore it. There was something about this last threat to Becky that made him feel uneasy. It was clear someone was following her movements very closely. How else had they known she'd be at the beach, sitting in that particular spot among a huge crowd? Jack knew the sooner he got her out of the city and into his house where he could keep an eye on her, the better. He also knew it would take every iota of self-control he possessed to keep his hands off her, but he'd never forgive himself if anything happened to her. If only Ben would contact him again! He wanted his advice on the cop Becky had met for a drink. What if *he* was the informant Ben had alluded to?

They drove to her flat in Randwick. He took her key to open the door, his eyes widening at the mess in front of them.

'It's not pretty, is it?' she said, giving one of her torn books a despondent kick with one foot.

'I think it might be best if you just take what you value for sentimental reasons and the rest can be replaced through insurance,' he said. 'Got any garbage bags?'

She nodded and went to get them out of the small kitchen, bending down to the floor where they'd been strewn along with all the rest of the items in the drawers. But before she could straighten back up a missile came crashing through the kitchen window, shattering the glass and landing right in front of her.

'Becky?' Jack rushed to the kitchen and saw her on the floor, her face totally white as she held a rock in her hand.

'What happened?' He stepped over the glass and helped her to her feet. 'Did that just come through the window?'

She nodded and silently handed him the piece of paper that had been attached to the rock with an elastic band. He looked down at it, his stomach tightening as he read what was written there.

GET OUT OR DIE

'Right,' he said, taking her hand and pulling her out of the room. 'Forget your stuff—we're leaving.'

'No!' She tugged on his hand. 'I'm sick of being terrorised. I'm going to get my things and if anyone wants to take a potshot at me, let them.'

'Are you *mad?*' He tightened his hold. 'You don't know who's behind this.'

'I don't care. I want my things and I'm not leaving until I get them.' She extracted herself from his grasp and dug into her bag for her phone.

'What are you doing?'

She gave him a determined look. 'I'm calling Matt Daniels, the cop who is working on the investigation.'

Jack felt sick. He watched as she dialled the direct number she read off a card but he couldn't think of a way to stop her that wouldn't make her even more suspicious.

'Constable Daniels.'

There was the sound of scuffling in the background but in her rush to speak to him Becky ignored it. 'Matt?' She turned her back towards Jack. 'It's Becky Baxter.'

'Hello, Becky.' There was the sound of a male grunt before he added, 'How are things?'

'I need to talk to you. I've had a couple of weird things happen just lately.'

There was a tiny pause before Matt spoke. 'Why don't we meet some time tomorrow? I'm a bit tied up today, but what about tomorrow evening? Can it wait until then?'

Becky worried her lip before answering, 'Sure, it can wait.'

'Are you still at the hotel?'

'No. I'll be staying with a family…er…friend.' She gave him Jack's address.

'I'll pick you up about seven, if that's all right. Maybe we could have dinner?' Matt said.

'Dinner would be very nice,' she answered with a defiant glance in Jack's direction. 'And seven is perfect.'

'Great, see you then.'

'Bye.'

Jack made a sound of disgust in the back of his throat.

'What?' Becky spun around to glare at him.

'If he's such a great cop, why isn't he high-tailing it round here right now instead of taking you out to dinner tomorrow?'

'You shouldn't listen in on other people's conversations,' she reprimanded him coldly. 'Anyway, I like him. He reminds me of Ben.'

'Anyone in police uniform reminds you of Ben. It doesn't mean they aren't corrupt.'

'Corrupt?' Her mouth dropped open. 'What makes you think Matt Daniels is corrupt?'

'He hardly knows you and here he is, taking you out.'

'Maybe he's seriously attracted to me.' She gave him a pointed look and added in a breathy little tone, 'Maybe he even wants to have sex with me.'

'Oh, for God's sake, you're surely not thinking about jumping into bed with him? You don't know anything about him!'

'I intend to get to know him,' she informed him determinedly. 'I haven't been on a proper date in ages and I'm looking forward to it.'

Jack closed his teeth with a snap and watched as she sorted through her things, his gut clenching at the thought of her going out with a man who might very well have murder on his mind.

It wasn't that he was jealous…

Of course he wasn't.

He wasn't the jealous type. He had never felt anything more than a casual interest in any woman so he didn't see why he should be feeling so edgy about Becky getting involved with a man who could after all be a nice enough guy. He had no proof that Constable Daniels wasn't above board. All Ben had said was to trust no one.

It had nothing to do with being jealous.

He clenched his jaw.

OK, so maybe he was a little bit jealous.

But it was just because he didn't like to think of her throwing her life away on someone not good enough for her. As Ben had said, she had lousy taste in men; she could easily be hoodwinked into yet another disastrous relationship.

It wasn't that he thought of her as a potential partner for himself...

He gave himself a mental shake but no matter how hard he tried he couldn't quite forget the feel of her mouth, not to mention the caress of her busy little fingers on his—

'I'm all done,' Becky announced, jarring him out of his reverie. 'Let's go.'

He looked at her blankly for a moment or two.

'Hello?' Becky waved her hand in front of his face. 'Anyone home in there?'

'What?' His throat moved up and down in a convulsive swallow.

'What planet were you just on?'

'Planet?'

She rolled her eyes at him. 'Earth to Jack, can you read me?'

'Yeah...go...sure, let's go.' He took the garbage bag and held open the door, his movements mechanical.

It came to him then as if he had indeed been occupying some other planet, where the truth had been concealed from him all this time. He had feelings for Becky Baxter that had absolutely nothing to do with his promise to Ben. Feelings that he'd spent most of his adulthood avoiding.

He drove back to his house in a shell-shocked silence. He was conscious of Becky sitting within touching distance but she may as well have been sitting on the other side of the earth. She had told him so many times how much she disliked im, and even though she'd obviously been tempted to sleep with him the evening before, he knew the alcohol she'd consumed had coloured her judgement. She'd told him as much.

He helped her inside with her things, keeping conversation to an absolute minimum. Once she was more or less settled back in the spare room he made some vague excuse about going to the hospital which he knew could have waited till morning, but he felt in dire need of some breathing space. He reassured himself that after this latest scare she wouldn't do another disappearing act, and if he was super-quick he'd be back within forty minutes, maybe before she even got out of the shower.

'Shall I organise something for us to eat for when you get back?' Becky offered as he made his way to the door.

'Not for me,' he said. 'I'm not hungry, but you go right ahead. Help yourself.'

Becky frowned as she watched him leave. There was something about Jack that didn't quite add up. He was all protective and concerned for her welfare one minute and the next he looked as if he couldn't wait to get away from her. She gave a dispirited sigh and looked at her things sitting on the bed, waiting to be unpacked.

Temporarily, she reminded herself with a sharp pang of regret. Jack didn't want her in his life on a permanent basis, and if it hadn't been for his friendship with Ben and her parents, she wouldn't be in at all.

HDU was full that night, all eight beds occupied with post-op cases, some elderly and frail and struggling to recover from routine surgery, others recuperating from major surgery. Jack had two patients there, a severe pancreatitic and the splenectomy with diaphragmatic repair from his recent list. Cindy Jones was special-nursing both his patients and as Jack arrived, Robert greeted him in his usual formal manner.

Jack gave a brief nod in reply and reached for the first patient's notes.

'How are they doing, Robert? Any major issues?'

'Mr Pearson, the pancreatitic, is oliguric, despite pretty vig orous fluid resus. His urine output is under 10 mls per hour His Ransom criteria are poor, he's not doing too well.'

'Have you got the CT report?'

'That's what I wanted to show you. They did fine slices through the pancreas with IV contrast. Most of the pancreas doesn't show up—I think he has major pancreatic necrosis.'

'Do they report any collection?'

'No collection, but a lot of peripancreatic oedema.'

'We may have to debride the pancreas. Can we get a Swan Ganz in and add in IV frusemide to try and up his urine out put?'

'He's too much for us in HDU, Mr Colcannon,' Cindy Jones put in. 'Can we get him transferred to ICU?'

'I'm inclined to agree with you, Cindy. The last lot of blood gases makes it look like ventilation is going to be needed. Can you speak to ICU, Robert? Get him transferred round there involve the intensivists, and we'll review the likelihood of sur gery in the morning.'

'I'll get on to it now, Mr Colcannon. The splenectomy is fine, needing a lot of physio on his left chest, but OK.'

'Thanks, Robert. You're doing a great job with these dif ficult cases.'

'Thanks, sir. I'll see you in the morning. Have a good eve ning.'

'Right,' Jack said, glancing at his watch. If he put his foo down he'd be home in record time.

Becky had finished a simple meal of cheese on toast and had not long stepped out of the shower when she heard the sound of Jack moving about downstairs.

She towelled her hair and called out to him, 'How were things at the hospital?'

He didn't answer and she sighed as she reached for the hairdryer and gave her head a quick blast.

OK, so he was still annoyed with her for arranging to meet Matt Daniels the following evening. She couldn't understand why he was being so dog-in-the-manger about it. Even though he'd kissed her he'd made it perfectly clear he had no interest in her personally. He even avoided looking at her unless he absolutely had to. She'd seen the way his green eyes flicked away whenever she asked him something lately.

She turned off the dryer and peered at herself in the mirror above the basin and sighed. Was she *that* unattractive? Sure, she had a couple of pounds to lose, but what girl with an incurable sweet tooth didn't? So, she didn't quite meet his exacting standards. So what? His ex-girlfriend Marcia hadn't exactly been an oil painting.

Actually, she had, Becky conceded with a twist to her mouth as she unplugged the dryer. Marcia was a hospital physiotherapist who had the sort of face and figure that made most women envious and all men drool.

But that was beside the point.

She put the hairdryer down with a snap. She had the right to date whoever she liked and if she wanted to go out with Matt Daniels then she would go and enjoy herself. It wasn't as if she was going to let it go any further. How could it, when she was in love with Jack?

There was another sound of movement downstairs and, tucking the towel around her chest sarong-wise, she opened the bathroom door and called out once more.

'Jack?'

The house was quiet.

Too quiet.

Becky felt the sharp edges of fear claw at her insides as she strained her ears, her heart starting to leap about in her chest.

Was that a footstep on the stairs?

A creaking floorboard?

She spun around for a weapon, her eyes going to the still warm hairdryer. She grabbed it in both hands, holding it in front of her like a gun.

This had gone on long enough.

She wasn't going to be found cowering behind the bathroom door, waiting for her attacker to seek her out. No way.

She was going to come out fighting.

She took a steadying breath and pushed open the bathroom door.

CHAPTER NINE

'WHAT the—?' Jack stumbled backwards in shock as something caught him a glancing blow to his head. White spots of light flashed before his eyes and he clutched for the wall to keep himself upright.

'*Ohmigod!*' Becky stared in horror at the blood spurting from a gash just above Jack's right eye. 'It's you!'

'Yeah, it's me.' His words came out sounding a little woozy but his tone was still unmistakably dry. 'Or at least it was until you half brained me.' He lifted his fingers up to inspect the damage, wincing as they came back down covered in blood. 'But who knows? This could bring on that personality bypass you've been insisting I need.'

'I think it needs stitching.' She caught her lip between her teeth.

'Well, you'd better do it,' he said, brushing past her to enter the bathroom. 'I have a weak stomach when it comes to blood.'

'Very funny.' She spun on her heel to join him in the bathroom, meeting his eyes in the mirror where he was examining the wound. 'D-does it hurt?'

'Only when I breathe.' He held a facecloth to it and turned around to look at her. 'What made you do it? I thought we'd agreed to call a truce.'

'I thought you were an intruder.' She suddenly realised she was still holding the hairdryer and put it down with a little clatter on the vanity top. 'You didn't answer when I called out to you.'

'I called out to you three times, but you had the dryer going,' he said.

'Oh.'

He turned back to the mirror and checked the bleeding. 'Can you get my doctor's bag? It's in my study downstairs. I don't want to drip blood all over the carpet.'

She made a quick detour to her room, tossing the towel aside as she slipped on her bathrobe, before going for his bag and bringing it back up.

'You'd better sit down on the toilet seat while I do this,' she instructed.

He did as she said and she opened the bag, conscious of his long legs right behind her. She rummaged in the kit and found some steristrips and dressings, and gave her knuckles a mental crack or two.

'Maybe I'll just steristrip it,' she said somewhat nervously. Treating a highly skilled surgeon when you didn't have any major surgical skills except for anaesthetic procedures was not to be recommended, Becky thought ruefully as she leaned forward.

Jack removed his hand from the facecloth he'd been pressing to stem the flow of blood, but there was still a significant trickle from the wound.

'It's still bleeding. Put some pressure on it for five minutes and it should stop.'

'Lean back a bit so I can push on it.' Becky grabbed a pad of gauze she'd found in the medical kit.

After what seemed like five hours instead of five minutes with his body so close to hers in the tight space, she removed the gauze, relieved the bleeding had stopped.

'It's dry. I'll steristrip it now.'

'I can do it myself by looking in the mirror.' Jack started to get up off the toilet seat but she put a hand on his shoulder and pressed him back down.

'I know it's been a while since I've done this,' she said, 'but surely you trust me?'

He gave her an ironic glance from beneath his lashes. 'I don't trust you at all, but I'm too embarrassed to rock up to A and E and tell whoever's on duty that I've been assaulted with a hairdryer in my very own house.'

Becky felt the colour surge in her cheeks as she reached for some antiseptic, soaking a pad generously before turning to apply it to his wound.

'*Ouch!*'

'Don't be such a baby,' she chided him, stepping between his spread thighs to get closer to his wound.

She was intensely conscious of her nakedness beneath her worn bathrobe, her skin suddenly feeling overly sensitive where it brushed the cotton with each tiny movement she made.

She took a prickly sort of breath and added, 'I would have thought you'd be a little braver, considering the amount of pain you inflict on some of your patients at times.'

He grunted something under his breath before grumbling, 'I hope you're not going to leave me with a Dr Frankenstein scar.'

'Will you shut up and let me concentrate?' She put the antiseptic to one side. 'I'm not used to patients speaking to me while I tend them.'

'Just as well.'

'Hold still,' she said. 'I don't want to make a mess of it. Is it still hurting?'

'Not really, but I've got the mother of all headaches.'

'You might be a little concussed.' She carefully applied the steristrips, making sure the edges of the wound were close together. 'You might also end up with a black eye but hopefully you won't need plastic surgery.'

'Thank God.'

'Want to have a look before I dress it?'

He got up from the toilet seat and looked at the row of neat butterfly strips over his eye. 'Not bad.'

'Wow, a compliment from Mr Perfect himself!' She unpeeled a sterile dressing and reached up to apply it to his head. 'Bend down a little,' she said. 'You're too tall… There, that's it.'

'Don't you think you should check my pupils for any irregularities?' Jack said.

She stood on tiptoe and peered into his eyes. His pupils were dilated, but evenly, his green eyes glittering with something…was it pain, or maybe something else?

The silence seemed to stretch like a piece of elastic that had been under too much pressure for too long.

Becky felt the magnetic pull of Jack's gaze and suddenly found it hard to breathe. The air felt too thick. It dragged at her chest and throat until she was sure she was going to pass out with the effort of inflating her lungs enough to speak.

'I—I'm so sorry.' She stumbled over her apology. 'I didn't expect you back so soon. I really thought you were an intruder.' She twisted her hands a little bit and went on to explain, 'I didn't want to hide away like a coward, waiting for him to strike me down. I thought I'd get in first.'

He gave her a look of incredulity. 'So you thought you'd take him on all by yourself with a *hairdryer*? What were you thinking?' He gave a snort of derision. 'You wouldn't stand a chance defending yourself.'

She lifted her chin. 'I caught *you* off guard. You went down like a ton of bricks.'

'I did not!'

'Yes, you did.' Her mouth kicked up in a tiny smile. 'You didn't even block my hit.'

He gave her a disdainful look. 'That's because I knew it was you.'

'Then why didn't you say something and stop me?'

'How could I? You came at me like a bull at a gate. Besides, I didn't want to hurt you. One decent block from me might have broken your arm.'

Deep down Becky knew he was right, although the very last thing she wanted to do was admit it. She'd flown at him in such a rush, not even stopping to check his identity. If he'd so much as put up his arm to block her attack, she would have bounced off him like a rubber ball off a brick wall. Her brief bout of bravery seemed rather pathetic now she looked back at it with hindsight.

'I'll get you some Panadeine,' she mumbled and started for his bag.

'I don't need them,' he said. 'I think I'll lie down for a while with a cold pack. I have a full list tomorrow and I don't want to be drugged up to the eyeballs.'

He moved past her and she began clearing away the mess, grimacing at the amount of blood on the pads she threw in the bin.

'How are you feeling this morning?' Becky asked the next morning as she came into the kitchen where Jack had his head bent over the newspaper.

He lifted his head to look at her.

'Oh, my God, your eye!' she gasped. 'It's totally black!'

'As you see,' he said, his tone clipped.

'The cold pack didn't work?'

'Apparently not.'

'I don't know what to say.'

'It's been my experience with you that least said is soonest mended,' he commented dryly as he reached for his coffee.

Becky pursed her mouth in sudden anger. How like him to want to make her feel even worse.

'I'm going to work,' she announced tersely.

His glance went to the clock on the wall before returning to her flashing eyes.

'A whole hour early?'

'Why not?' She folded her arms crossly. 'You do it every day.'

'How are you intending on getting there?' He quirked one dark brow at her over the rim of his coffee-cup.

'I—' She snapped her mouth closed. She'd forgotten all about her car.

'Come on,' he said, pushing his cup aside. 'I'm ready to leave now anyway.'

'I'd rather walk.'

He gave her one of his don't-push-me-too-far looks as he scooped up his keys.

'Want to have a rethink on that, Becky?'

She pushed past him in the doorway, her colour high and her temper even higher.

'I should have hit you harder when I had the chance,' she snapped at him spitefully.

'Just try it, sweetheart, and see how far it gets you.'

Becky didn't answer. That funny flickering pulse had settled between her thighs once more, making her feel as if he had reached out and touched her intimately. She swung away and stalked out of the room, but even twenty minutes later as they drove in to the hospital in a mutually agreed stiff silence, she could still feel it beating within her.

Becky had the first patient—Mr Bamford, for an incisional hernia repair—on the table and asleep before Jack had even emerged from the change room.

'What happened to you?' Gwen gaped as Jack pushed through the theatre doors, arms upturned after his first scrub.

'I ran into something in the dark last night,' Jack mumbled from behind his mask. 'Just a little cut but the bruising has given me a black eye.'

'Gosh, it looks gross.'

Jack sent Becky a speaking glance before turning to Gwen. 'Thanks, but it looks much worse than it feels, I can assure you. Prep, please.'

He prepped the abdomen, applied the steridrape and set up the diathermy and sucker while Robert gowned.

'We're using mesh, Dr Baxter. Can you give a gram of cephalosporin?'

'Yes. I've got it mixed, it'll go through in a sec,' Becky answered, without looking at him.

Jack made a vertical incision and freed up and reduced the hernia.

'Let's have the 12 by 12 centimetre polypropylene mesh, Gwen, please, and lots of one-nylon sutures.'

'Do you want me to clip those, or cut as we go?' Robert asked.

'Cut, thanks, Robert, about a centimetre long. We need big bites and no tension.'

For the next twenty minutes Jack sutured in the mesh patch, trimming it to match the size of the hernia neck as he went.

'One-sixty milligrams gentamicin for the wound please, Gwen.'

'Will you use a drain, Mr Colcannon?' asked Robert.

'No, I don't use drains in this situation. Seroma formation is common, but there is no evidence that drains prevent it.' Jack suggested a couple of reviews for Robert to consult as he closed the wound with staples.

Jack was just finishing up the next routine case, a laparoscopic gall bladder, when Robert's page went off. 'Unscrub, Robert. I'll put in the skin sutures. You'd better get that page,' he said as he removed the last of the laparoscopic ports.

'Thanks, Mr Colcannon, I think that's a code blue for an emergency in A and E.'

Robert moved to the back of the theatre to use the theatre phone, but within a couple of minutes he was back at the operating table, looking a little pale.

'What's the problem?' Jack asked as Becky accompanied the patient out to recovery.

'There's a ruptured triple-A downstairs, confirmed on CT. He needs Theatre now. They want to break into our list—all the other theatres are in the middle of cases,' Robert informed him.

'*Shoot!*' Jack gritted his teeth in frustration. 'That's going to take three hours at least. We may as well forget about the rest of our list.'

'I'm afraid that's not the worst news, Mr Colcannon.'

'I can't imagine what's worse than having my elective list screwed up with a ruptured triple-A. Some of these patients have been waiting months for surgery, now I have to hand over my valuable theatre time to the vascular guys.'

'Well, actually…' Robert said with a grimace. 'All three vascular surgeons are away at a conference, and general surgery is covering vascular cases.'

'Oh, great,' Jack said darkly. 'I didn't get a memo from Admin about that. I wonder who the poor guy on call is who's going to have to deal with that?'

'Yes, well, that's the rest of the message,' Robert said.

Jack gave him a narrow-eyed look. 'You're kidding me, right?'

The registrar shook his head. 'You're on call for general surgery today.'

'I can't be on call again. Triple-A? I haven't done an elective triple-A since my registrar training, let alone a ruptured triple-A.'

Robert's pager beeped a text message and he read it out loud, '''Patient's in the lift, on his way up, with eight units of blood.'''

'This is totally ridiculous!' Jack raised his voice. 'I'm being shafted into doing an operation I'm not properly trained for because the idiotic administration let all three vascular surgeons go on leave at the same time, and then tell me at the last minute that I'm covering.'

Becky could hear the shouting from the recovery room, where she had just taken the last patient. She had just been told of the situation by the recovery staff, and as she was the only free anaesthetist right now, she knew she was going to have to anaesthetise the triple-A. Theatre staff had already moved into action and were quickly setting up for a vascular case.

The lift doors burst open and two nurses and the A and E senior resident wheeled the desperately ill patient straight down the corridor toward Theatre.

Becky took over bagging and masking the patient and proceeded into Theatre, the orderlies transferring him across to the operating table. She administered high-flow oxygen while the anaesthetic nurse continued to pump in blood through the drip. Becky injected and intubated the patient, and connected him to the anaesthetic machine. She helped pump in blood through two drips as the monitor warned her of hypotension.

Jack burst through the theatre door, having scrubbed and

rapidly gowned while Gwen had set up the vascular instrument pack.

'You've got to clamp that aorta, Jack,' Becky said urgently. 'I've got no blood pressure up this end.'

'Rapid prep and drape, Gwen,' Jack said tightly.

Robert assisted with the set-up, and Jack made a long midline incision in the abdomen. The distended abdomen suddenly exploded with a gush of several litres of bright red blood.

'Aortic clamp!' Jack shouted, as he positioned Robert's hands with packs. He rapidly positioned the clamp across the aorta and squeezed hard on the handles, but the massive blood loss continued unabated.

'What the hell? The aorta won't clamp. It's rigid with calcification!'

Becky's anaesthetic machine gave a long monotonous beep.

'He's arrested, Jack. I've got no blood pressure and he's in asystole.'

In desperation Jack opened the aneurysm sac, scooped out plaque and clot from the calcified aneurysm sac, and shoved his left index finger into the lumen of the aorta. But the brittle vessel simply split further, releasing a final few surges of bright red blood before even that stopped, Becky's machine screaming the message that the patient had bled out and had no more blood to pump around.

In spite of twenty minutes of external cardiac massage, intracardiac adrenalin and massive volume replacement, with Jack finally managing to clamp the aorta, but above the renals, Becky gave the bad news.

'I'm stopping resus, Jack. He's gone, and nothing's going to restart this heart.'

Becky watched as Jack stood perfectly still for a moment or two, his gloved hands and gown covered in the patient's blood, his eyes behind his protective shield staring down at the lifeless body on the table.

'It was calcified,' she said. 'No one could have clamped it.'

Jack stripped off his gloves and gown and tossed them aside, his head gear soon following, his expression grim.

'You did the best you could do,' she added to fill the awkward silence. 'No one can ask more than that.'

Jack's hard green gaze hit hers with the full force of his bitter disappointment. 'Somehow I don't think that's going to comfort this man's wife and family, is it, Dr Baxter? That I tried my best?'

Becky opened her mouth to respond but closed it when she saw the rigid set of his jaw. He was upset, and rightly so.

No one wanted to fail in an emergency, especially an emergency that had been thrust upon him with no time for him to prepare. And now he had the unenviable task of going out and meeting the patient's relatives to deliver the bad news, a task no doctor ever felt up to no matter how many years of experience he or she had gathered over their career.

Becky had seen it so many times it made her feel ill to think of what he had to face—the sea of expectant faces, small bright fragments of hope shining among the shadows of their eyes as they rose from the edges of the waiting-room chairs, the smell of half-drunk tea and coffee lingering in the air, along with the scent of gut-wrenching fear.

CHAPTER TEN

THE rest of the list resumed after the theatre was cleaned, but the usual conversation among the theatre staff gradually ceased as they witnessed Jack's brooding silence as he worked his way through the routine cases.

Becky felt sorry for Robert, who had a tendency to try too hard at the best of times. Now, with Jack's added tension, it seemed the registrar couldn't do a thing right.

'Robert, I'm off the screen. I can't do laparoscopic surgery unless you hold the camera on what I'm doing,' Jack clipped out tersely.

'Sorry, the other instruments seem to be clashing with the camera.'

'Look, just hold it still. If I knock the camera, just keep watching the screen and keep me in the middle of it,' Jack snapped back.

Robert kept trying to point the camera where he thought Jack wanted to look, but in the end Jack pushed and pulled the camera into position himself, telling the registrar in a hard tone to just hold the thing still.

Becky gave Jack a reproving look as a cowed-looking Robert left the tearoom after the list was finished.

'You didn't have to be so hard on him. I think he's doing a good job, considering the piecemeal cases he gets from the other surgeons,' she said.

Jack thrust his coffee-cup down with a sharp crack on the table.

'He needs to toughen up or he'll never survive the training scheme. He simpers about, showing no confidence at all. No patient is going to take to him unless he demonstrates his

111

ability to think and speak clearly, take some initiative and show some confidence.'

'You're hardly helping the process if you have him on tenterhooks all the time,' she pointed out. 'Everyone understands this afternoon's death was difficult, but I don't think it's fair to take it out on him.'

Jack's eyes glittered with sparks of anger as they pinned hers. 'What would you know? You weren't the one who had to face his wife, two daughters and three young grandchildren.'

'That must have been awful.'

He sucked in a ragged breath and turned away from her empathetic gaze.

'They had such hope in their eyes.' He moved across to the window and stared out over the hospital car park, his back turned towards her. 'I hate that—the way they look at you as if you are coming to tell them everything's gone well and he'll be up and about in a couple of hours for a cup of tea and a plate of sandwiches. Everyone expects miracles.' He swung around to look at her, his bruised eye looking all the more obvious with the shadows of disappointment in his gaze. 'It really gets to me. I always feel like the bloody Grim Reaper.'

'Jack—'

He held up his hand. 'No, don't insult me by saying it again. I don't need to hear I did my best, because you and I both know my best wasn't nearly good enough.'

'I wasn't going to say that.'

He gave her a long, hard look. 'What were you going to say?'

She stepped towards him and took one of his hands in hers, her small fingers stroking the long tanned length of his as she looked up into his face.

'I was going to say you are one hell of a surgeon and that if I ever had a surgical emergency you'd be the only one I'd want to help me.'

He held her look for a long time before speaking, his eyes, slightly misted, holding hers.

'Let's hope you won't be ever needing me that way,' he finally said, his tone a little rusty.

'I'm not planning on it, but I guess you never know, do you?' she said.

He didn't answer. Instead, he lifted his hand and traced one long finger down the curve of her cheek in a caress so soft Becky thought she must have imagined it.

'What was that for?' she asked, her voice a soft thread of sound.

He held her gaze for a long moment.

'Jack?'

He stepped back from her, his expression closing over, effectively shutting her out. 'I'll be ready to drive you home in about ten minutes. I just want to speak to someone first. I'll meet you at the front desk.' He turned and left the room, the door swinging shut behind him.

Becky turned and stared at his discarded cup on the table, and before she could stop herself she reached for it, running her fingertip around the rim where his lips had been, her mouth tingling in remembrance of how it had felt to have those lips pressed hard against hers.

Jack found Robert in the change room, gathering his things from his locker.

'I'll do a ward round now, Mr Colcannon, and ring you at home if any more emergencies come in.'

'No, you won't. Robert, you've got the potential to make a good surgeon. You did well this afternoon to cope with my mood after I lost that patient. I hope you're never in that situation but the odds are at some time you will be. It goes with the territory, I'm afraid, especially in the public system. But you look tired, and you should go home. I'll see the post-ops myself. Let A and E know they can reach you at home, and go get a break. I won't be far behind you. I'm more than a little bushed myself.'

'Thanks, sir.' Robert gave him a grateful glance. 'I was beginning to doubt myself this afternoon.'

'Don't be crazy, Robert. You're fine, just lacking in experience, which can easily be remedied. Now, get out of here. The place won't fall down without you.'

Jack allowed himself one small inaudible sigh as the registrar left the change room a short time later.

In some ways Robert reminded him of himself when he'd first started out—eager to please, wanting to learn as much as possible and be the sort of surgeon everyone had full confidence in. It only took a few losses to erode that growing confidence and he knew some trainees never quite recovered from it.

Losing patients was part of the cycle of a surgeon's life; even routine operations could go wrong. The human body, for all that science had discovered about it, still held some surprises. All one could hope for was that the cause of death was brought on by natural causes as the result of a disease going too far before treatment had occurred to try to stall the process. That was often true in the very elderly who had left things a little too long before having checks carried out. By the time they came to see him he had the loathsome task of offering them an operation that would very likely kill them or suggesting doing nothing, which would achieve exactly the same end. There had been some talk of rationing care in the public system—that expectations were too high, and that it couldn't provide maximal care to everyone.

Trauma, of course, was different. That was when good technical skill and a perfectly clear head in the 'golden hour' were vitally important. You still had your losses, inevitably, and often the recovery of those who did actually make it was long and arduous, some never making it back to full health.

It was times like these that he truly envied his father. Emery Colcannon hadn't lost a patient in the thirty years or so he'd been operating as a cosmetic surgeon, and never missed an opportunity to remind Jack of it. Jack had to make himself refrain from chipping back with some pithy comment about the dangers of getting it wrong with a Botox injection or eyelid lift hardly comparing with category-one trauma surgery.

Jack often wondered how his mother had survived living with his father as long as she had. He could stand about five minutes; she had survived eleven years, although she had barely spoken a word to her ex-husband since their divorce when Jack had been ten.

Jack knew his relationships with women were directly influenced by the bitter interactions between his parents. He hated feeling vulnerable in a relationship and had never allowed himself to feel anything other than physical desire with any of his previous partners.

But Becky was something else.

For years he had seen her as the kid sister of his best mate, almost wilfully blocking out the attraction he felt for her, in case he was tempted to act on it.

Damn it, but he was tempted.

Had been since that day he'd hauled her young supple body up against his and kissed her. And it hadn't been just a simple exploratory kiss, but the full works. The whole tongue routine, the pelvis against pelvis thing, and his hand on the soft budding breast, which he could still feel against his palm even after all these years.

He closed his hand into a fist a couple of times but the sensation was still there, as if the essence of Becky had eased itself beneath the surface of his skin, never to come out.

Even his house felt different now. He could sense her presence in every room and not just from her natural untidiness, which drove him crazy. It wasn't just the squashed cushions on the sofa where she'd been curled up or the damp towels hung up crookedly in the bathroom, or the scattered cosmetics containers with some of the lids still off. It wasn't even her perfume, which lingered in the air long after she'd left a room.

It felt to him as if by simply entering his house her lively personality had invaded the austere formal décor and somehow rearranged it permanently.

She was waiting for him at the front desk, chatting with the woman on duty as if they were old friends. Jack deliberately slowed his steps so he could watch her undetected. Her laughing brown eyes were sparkling with amusement, her soft mouth smiling, but her smile instantly faded when she turned her head and saw him. Jack couldn't help feeling annoyed, and to disguise his hurt he adopted a gruff demeanour as he led the way out to where his car was parked.

'What were you talking to the switchboard operator about?' he asked.

'Nothing.'

He gave her a disbelieving look as he unlocked his car. 'I would prefer it if you wouldn't discuss me with the hospital staff.'

'I wasn't discussing you,' Becky said. 'I was telling June about my date tonight.'

Jack's stomach gave a painful lurch. With all the stress of the day he'd forgotten all about her date with the cop. He drummed his fingers on the steering-wheel, wondering if he could come up with a good enough reason to get her to change her plans.

'And don't even think about trying to talk me out of it,' Becky said, giving him a warning glance. 'I've been looking forward to it all day.'

Jack didn't trust himself to respond. Instead, he concentrated fiercely on driving home, his mouth set in lines of tension as his mind raced with a thousand gut-wrenching scenarios.

'Jack, can you help me with my zipper?' Becky came bursting into the lounge room half an hour later. 'I think it's jammed or something.'

Jack sucked in a breath at the sight of her. She was dressed in a close-fitting ice-blue sheath that brought out the sun-kissed perfection of her skin and showcased her cleavage a little too well. She turned her back and his eyes widened at the slim length of her back, his fingers aching to trace a pathway down the delicate vertebrae.

'Can you see what's wrong with it?' she asked. 'Matt will be here any minute and I haven't even done my hair.'

'Um…' Jack's normally rock-steady hands started to tremble as he worked on the zipper, his knuckles brushing against her warm bare skin.

'I think I can see what's wrong,' he finally managed to say. 'It's caught on a little thread. Hold still while I unpick it.'

The doorbell sounded just as he slid the zipper up the length of her spine.

'Oh, no!' she gasped, spinning around to face him. 'Will you be a honey and let Matt in while I rush upstairs to do my hair?'

Jack grimaced as she bolted for the stairs. He drew in a breath and made his way to the front door, suddenly feeling about a hundred years old.

'Hi, I'm Matt Daniels.'

'Jack Colcannon.' Jack shook the other man's hand and in doing so tried to assess his character. The cop's grip was firm without being aggressive, his eye contact comfortably at ease, not in the least furtive or hesitant.

'So you're the family friend,' Matt said pleasantly.

'Yep, that's me.' Jack's tone was wry as he closed the door once Matt had entered the house.

Jack waited until they'd both moved through to the lounge before asking, 'Would you like a drink? Becky is probably going to be ages.'

'No, no drink, thank you.' Matt smiled and added, 'You know her very well, don't you?'

Jack found himself checking to see if the cop's smile made it the full distance to his eyes. It did.

'Yeah, you could say that.'

'You know her brother?'

Jack couldn't really tell from Matt's tone if he'd stated a fact or asked a question. It was a little disquieting, but cops were cops and he'd seen the same trait in Ben a thousand times.

'We were at the same boarding school,' he answered after a tiny pause. 'I used to spend a lot of holiday time at the Baxters' property in the southern highlands.'

'Mr and Mrs Baxter are currently overseas, aren't they?'

'Yes.'

The cop's eyes never once wavered from his, making Jack feel as if he was being cross-examined.

'What about her brother?' Matt asked casually. 'Any idea of where he is right now?'

Jack could feel his hackles rising and did his best to settle them back down.

'No.'

'So you haven't had any contact with him recently?' Matt's gaze seemed very direct and cop-like.

'No.'

'What happened to your eye?'

'I ran into a door.'

Jack could tell Matt didn't believe him but was saved from having to continue the conversation by Becky's arrival.

'I'm so sorry to have kept you waiting, Matt,' she said as she came into the room.

Both men turned to face her and she saw the male appreciation in both gazes as they swept over her, Jack's eyes in particular widening as they came to rest on the upthrust of her breasts.

Good.

It gave her a delicious feeling of power to know she affected him even though she could see he was doing his level best to hide it.

'Shall we go?' She hooked her arm through Matt's and turned towards Jack, sending him an arch look. 'You don't have to wait up. I'll let myself in.'

'I have some paperwork to see to anyway,' he said stiffly. 'I won't be going to bed early.'

'We won't be late,' Matt said. 'I have an early shift in the morning.'

Jack stretched his lips over clenched teeth. 'Have a wonderful time.'

'We will,' Becky said, and ushered her date to the door.

Jack waited until they were in the car before slipping out

to the garage to his own, starting it as quietly as he could and nudging it out to follow the cop's car at a discreet distance.

'I can't believe I'm doing this,' he muttered as he shifted through the gears. 'You owe me, Ben Baxter. Big time.'

As Matt drove to the restaurant strip of Glebe, Becky yet again couldn't help noticing the similarities he shared with Ben. He drove exactly the same way, his eyes repeatedly flicking to the rear-view mirror before darting to the right-hand driver's mirror.

'Jack seems to take his family friend status quite seriously,' Matt observed as he checked the mirrors again. 'Are you two involved in any way?'

'No, not really.' Becky fiddled with the strap of her evening purse.

'But you'd like to be?' Matt guessed, swinging a quick glance in her direction.

Becky gave him a shamefaced look. 'You must think I'm awful, accepting a date with you when I'm in love with someone else.'

Matt gave her a reassuring smile as he parked the car. 'You are one hell of an attractive lady, Becky, but to tell you the truth, every time you bat your eyelashes at me, you remind me of my kid sister.'

'That's really spooky,' she said. 'I was just thinking of how much you remind me of my brother.'

She stepped out of the car onto the pavement as he opened the door for her. 'So you don't mind if we just have dinner?' she asked.

He gave her another one of his easygoing smiles. 'That's fine by me. Come on, I'm starving.'

Once the waiter had left with their orders Matt leaned forward in his chair so that his forearms were resting on the table.

'So what did you want to tell me when you called yesterday? I'm sorry I couldn't speak to you right there and then but I was in the middle of something a little tricky.' His mouth tilted upwards in a dry little smile as he explained, 'I was handcuffed to a suspect, actually, and he wasn't too keen on being up close and personal with me.'

'Oh.' She recalled the scuffling sounds and gave a mental grimace.

'You said some weird stuff had happened,' he prompted.

Becky gave the straw in her glass a little twirl as she told him what had happened at the beach and later at the flat when the rock had come through the window.

'So both notes were handwritten, right?' Matt queried.

'Yes, black felt-tip pen, sort of smudged as if it had been scrawled in a hurry.'

'Do you still have both items?'

'Yes.'

'And you're positive you didn't see anyone loitering around your bag on the beach?'

'I was too busy with the woman who was having the hypo. There were people everywhere—you probably know what it's like when something like that happens. Swarms of people hang about, getting in the way.'

'Yes, unfortunately, I'm all too familiar with the pattern.' Matt took a sip of his drink before continuing, 'What about Jack? Did he see anything?'

'No.' She gave her straw another twirl, her eyes downcast for a moment. 'Actually, he didn't even want me to call the police.'

'Oh, really?' Matt's tone had gone all cop-like again. 'Do you have any idea why he would react in that way?'

She shook her head, raising her eyes to his once more. 'No. He's been acting so...so...' She hunted vainly for a word to describe Jack's behaviour of late.

'Weird?' Matt offered.

'Not really, just sort of more uptight and edgy than usual.'

'Have you considered the possibility that Jack might be in some way involved in the things that have been happening to you?' Matt asked.

Becky gaped at him for a moment. 'You can't be serious!